D

MW00617344

I hope this gives you a laugh!

Sarah

Unpronounceable

Conversation Pieces

A Small Paperback Series from Aqueduct Press
Subscriptions available: www.aqueductpress.com

1. The Grand Conversation
   Essays by L. Timmel Duchamp

2. With Her Body
   Short Fiction by Nicola Griffith

3. Changeling
   A Novella by Nancy Jane Moore

4. Counting on Wildflowers
   An Entanglement by Kim Antieau

5. The Traveling Tide
   Short Fiction by Rosaleen Love

6. The Adventures of the Faithful Counselor
   A Narrative Poem by Anne Sheldon

7. Ordinary People
   A Collection by Eleanor Arnason

8. Writing the Other
   A Practical Approach
   by Nisi Shawl & Cynthia Ward

9. Alien Bootlegger
   A Novella by Rebecca Ore

10. The Red Rose Rages (Bleeding)
    A Short Novel by L. Timmel Duchamp

11. Talking Back: Epistolary Fantasies
    edited by L. Timmel Duchamp

12. Absolute Uncertainty
    Short Fiction by Lucy Sussex

13. Candle in a Bottle
    A Novella by Carolyn Ives Gilman

14. Knots
      Short Fiction by Wendy Walker

15. Naomi Mitchison: A Profile of Her Life and Work
      A Monograph by Lesley A. Hall

16. We, Robots
      A Novella by Sue Lange

17. Making Love in Madrid
      A Novella by Kimberly Todd Wade

18. Of Love and Other Monsters
      A Novella by Vandana Singh

19. Aliens of the Heart
      Short Fiction by Carolyn Ives Gilman

20. Voices From Fairyland:
      The Fantastical Poems of Mary Coleridge, Charlotte
      Mew, and Sylvia Townsend Warner
      Edited and With Poems by Theodora Goss

21. My Death
      A Novella by Lisa Tuttle

22. De Secretis Mulierum
      A Novella by L. Timmel Duchamp

23. Distances
      A Novella by Vandana Singh

24. Three Observations and a Dialogue:
      Round and About SF
      Essays by Sylvia Kelso and a correspondence
      with Lois McMaster Bujold

25. The Buonarotti Quartet
      Short Fiction by Gwyneth Jones

26. Slightly Behind and to the Left
      Four Stories & Three Drabbles by Claire Light

27. Through the Drowsy Dark
      Short Fiction and Poetry
      by Rachel Swirsky

28. Shotgun Lullabies
      Stories and Poems by Sheree Renée Thomas

29. A Brood of Foxes
    A Novella by Kristin Livdahl

30. The Bone Spindle
    Poems and Short Fiction by Anne Sheldon

31. The Last Letter
    A Novella by Fiona Lehn

32. We Wuz Pushed
    On Joanna Russ and Radical Truth-Telling
    by Brit Mandelo

33. The Receptionist and Other Tales
    Poems by Lesley Wheeler

34. Birds and Birthdays
    Stories by Christopher Barzak

35. The Queen, the Cambion, and Seven Others
    Stories by Richard Bowes

36. Spring in Geneva
    A Novella by Sylvia Kelso

37. The XY Conspiracy
    A Novella by Lori Selke

38. Numa
    An Epic Poem
    by Katrinka Moore

39. Myths, Metaphors, and Science Fiction:
    Ancient Roots of the Literature of the Future
    Essays by Sheila Finch

40. NoFood
    Short Fiction by Sarah Tolmie

41. The Haunted Girl
    Poems and Short Stories by Lisa M. Bradley

42. Three Songs for Roxy
    A Novella by Caren Gussoff

43. Ghost Signs
    Poems and a Short Story by Sonya Taaffe

44. The Prince of the Aquamarines & The Invisible
    Prince: Two Fairy Tales
    by Louise Cavelier Levesque

45. Back, Belly, and Side: True Lies and False Tales
    by Celeste Rita Baker

46. A Day in Deep Freeze
    A Novella by Lisa Shapter

47. A Field Guide to the Spirits
    Poems by Jean LeBlanc

48. Marginalia to Stone Bird
    Poems by Rose Lemberg

49. Unpronounceable
    A Novella by Susan diRende

50. Sleeping Under the Tree of Life
    Poems and Stories by Sheree Renée Thomas

About the Aqueduct Press
Conversation Pieces Series

The feminist engaged with sf is passionately interested in challenging the way things are, passionately determined to understand how everything works. It is my constant sense of our feminist-sf present as a grand conversation that enables me to trace its existence into the past and from there see its trajectory extending into our future. A genealogy for feminist sf would not constitute a chart depicting direct lineages but would offer us an ever-shifting, fluid mosaic, the individual tiles of which we will probably only ever partially access. What could be more in the spirit of feminist sf than to conceptualize a genealogy that explicitly manifests our own communities across not only space but also time?

Aqueduct's small paperback series, Conversation Pieces, aims to both document and facilitate the "grand conversation." The Conversation Pieces series presents a wide variety of texts, including short fiction (which may not always be sf and may not necessarily even be feminist), essays, speeches, manifestoes, poetry, interviews, correspondence, and group discussions. Many of the texts are reprinted material, but some are new. The grand conversation reaches at least as far back as Mary Shelley and extends, in our speculations and visions, into the continually-created future. In Jonathan Goldberg's words, "To look forward to the history that will be, one must look at and retell the history that has been told." And that is what Conversation Pieces is all about.

L. Timmel Duchamp

Jonathan Goldberg, "The History That Will Be" in Louise Fradenburg and Carla Freccero, eds., *Premodern Sexualities* (New York and London: Routledge, 1996)

Published by Aqueduct Press
PO Box 95787
Seattle, WA 98145-2787
www.aqueductpress.com

10 9 8 7 6 5 4 3 2 1
ISBN: 978-1-61976-107-0

Cover illustration courtesy Susan diRende

Original Block Print of Mary Shelley by Justin Kempton:
www.writersmugs.com
Printed in the USA by Applied Digital Imaging

Conversation Pieces
Volume 49

Unpronounceable

by
Susan diRende

To all the fierce and funny women in my life: my mother, big sisters, grandmothers, nieces, collaborators, and friends.

Chapter 1
Diplomatic Impunity

I wouldn't never have left New Jersey, let alone the planet Earth, if it wasn't for my sister, Alice, who you should know up front got all the genetic engineering bonus points my parents was assigned, leaving me with whatever they could come up with naturally, sperm-and-eggwise. Considering the DNA that was brought to a certain Christmas party exactly twenty-eight years and nine months before my last birthday, I consider myself lucky to have a full set of body parts and smarts enough not to get run over by a bus.

It all started when Alice made that crack about how Rose—that's me—wasn't going anywhere with her life. I get this on top of my boyfriend, Bob, sleeping with the landlady in my bed on my purple satin sheets that I had bought to seduce him with (which worked like a charm and hence him being my boyfriend). Excuse me, ex-boyfriend, because walking in on him making like the Little-Train-That-Could with her reminded me that I do have some pride, even though Bob possesses the kind of washboard pecs that can make a girl forget sometimes, and I told him to remove his rubber ducky from the premises.

I knew I also had to prevent Bob from ever wanting me to take him back, because with his build and his flawless self-absorption, me, I'd probably do it, Landlady Moss and her circus skills notwithstanding. So, only to protect myself from myself, not for the pleasure of telling a man the truth about sex for once, I let him in on a few of his personal inadequacies, including those regarding the size and shape of his favorite toy.

I must have laid it on good, because he's so mad he goes and tells the landlord a thing or two, not about the basement Barnum-and-Bailey performances with the missus, oh no, but about Rose—me again—having an illegal sublet in his rent-controlled apartment. Can you beat that?

So there I am, admiring Bob's killer instinct enough to miss him, which shows you the wisdom of my earlier pre-emptive thermonuclear verbiage, and having no place to live right when my period is due.

Meanwhile, the government has been sending one embarrassment to humanity after another to be Earth's Ambassador to the planet of the Unpronounceable (don't ask me to say it) until the United Nations gives up and figures anybody will do. *Anybody.* Be honest, do I sound like a diplomat to you?

The French, they invented diplomacy, send the French, I say. But no. That French guy that went looks like Pepe Le Pew on that old cartoon. Le Pew, the skunk, spends ten days on their world and it's back to the Eiffel Tower with him. The General, the one after Frenchie, four stars and he comes home with a nervous breakdown. The Japanese guy kills himself, so I guess that makes him the only diplomat that wasn't actually sent back in disgrace.

They figure maybe the Unpronounceable don't like diplomatic types. They try a businessman. Disaster. They try a poet. Didn't even know he was on another planet. They pick a whole Crayola assortment of doctors, scientists, anthropologists, philosophers, you know, bright but messy. The group lasts a whole month before they come back home with a note pinned to their collective collar asking us not to use their planet as an insane asylum. The Unpronounceable would welcome any sane person, but please to stop with the nut cases.

This poses a problem for the government. Should they just admit to our first interplanetary contacts that all of humanity was insane? Never.

So, the bureaucrats start thinking. Well not really thinking, but they think they're thinking. They figure if all sensible criteria pick somebody the aliens call crazy, then crazy criteria just might pick a winner. The United Nations go for the dumbest way to pick a representative of the human race and come up ace—a Lottery. I mean, think about it. Who wins lotteries?

A big announcement gets made all over the world. Anybody who wants to be humankind's envoy to the only extraterrestrial sentient race discovered in a hundred worlds could just put their name in a hat, no questions asked. The space program gets what they want. Wackos. Evangelists. People too dumb to see it's a set-up so's there'll be some lunatic to blame for messing up interplanetary relations for the rest of us. Nobody in their right mind would go near the thing.

See, now you're wondering about me. The only reason I put my name in at all was because Alice made that crack at the dinner table the very day the announcement of the Lottery came out. I'm thinking anyplace still in the same solar system with Alice is not far enough to count as going anywhere, and this is why I never made the effort. Unpronounceable would put over a thousand light-years of interstellar void between me and my sister. I announced my decision to apply right after the minestrone.

I was reckless, but hey, the odds against me being chosen were more than Einstein could figure. Besides, I never win anything. Anything good, I should have remembered, because I did win that fish in fourth grade that died on the way home, and I had to listen to a lecture from Nonna about how I was going to Hell for murdering one of God's creatures.

The point being, I'm not exactly happy when the name that pops up out of the gazillion of nudniks who actually do want to go is mine: Rosalba Bellicosa Delancy, Italian/Irish, actress/waitress, three-semester community college dropout, two serious boyfriends, both history; just your ordinary

American gal having a dry spell in romance, acting jobs, luck. It's not like I'd be leaving anything special.

Still, I try to get out of it. "I can't go up in a rocket. I'm afraid of heights."

"No, no it's not like that at all, Rose. More like being in an elevator," they tell me. I should've said I was afraid of elevators. How was I to know?

Unpronounceable is even further out from the center of the galaxy you and I call the Milky Way than Hackensack is from Heaven. To get there, the ships do some funny folding stuff with space and time, so that instead of the trip taking thousands of years, in which case everybody you went to school with would be dead, which if you ask me would be an incentive to go, but no, you get there in a couple of days. Actually, it only seems like a couple of days, because time is all screwed up and apparently anywhere from a week to nine months passes on Earth. It depends on the Fold, they say. I say I want to live my life the old-fashioned way, one day at a time, but nobody laughs.

You'd think this would be my shining hour. The problem is that when all the news hounds converge on our house, those cameras take one look at my sister and suddenly she's showing up in more interviews than me. It's no fun knowing the entire world agrees that, "Alice got the looks and brains, but Rose got more than her share of," —and here you have to do Aunt Mizi's now-famous roll of the eyes— "personality."

I have to admit it was good to get away. There's a crew on the ship, but they just shake their heads at me all sad and sorry, and leave me alone.

One guy, Maurice, he tries to explain their attitude has more to do with the aliens than me, so I shouldn't take it personal. Like I cared. Actually, I think Maurice is kind of sweet on me, which makes him even less interesting. He wants to warn me, he says.

Too late, I say. I'm stuck with going and making a fool of myself in front of the whole planet Earth, not to mention my Aunt Mizi, whose idea of a good story is some humiliating experience her dearly beloveds have brought on themselves, which she proceeds to tell every human she meets on the bus, in line at the grocery store, or panhandling on the street. Gotta love her, or she'd be dead.

Maurice says no, not warn me about Earth, but about the aliens, how the public don't know, but they are sadists who torture people for fun. Maurice puts his nubby fingertip on my shoulder and leans in close enough for me to smell his breath mint and write him off my dance card forever. "You must never go to a [*spitting-choking-word*]."

"Gesundheit," I say back.

"No, no. A [*spitting-choking-word*] is some kind of torture chamber. Both of the guys who went to one had to have emergency medical care on the return ship because all their skin was gone. They looked like pulsing globs of bloody red meat."

I feel my neck and armpits get clammy as my stomach has second thoughts about lunch. I know humans have blood inside of them, but I don't like to think about it. When I first started getting my period, I used to faint on the toilet until I learned how to use tampons with my eyes shut and the bathroom light off.

I try to put on a good face in front of Maurice. If I started crying, he'd want to kiss me, dontcha know, and what with my heaving stomach already, that wouldn't turn out too good. So I say I grew up in New Jersey and am experienced in handling sadists. He laughs and feels better, I guess. At least he don't make a pass. Me, I go to my cabin and spend an hour trying not to throw up. I fail.

See, I am not brave. I am stupid, which sometimes makes me look brave, but there's a big difference. Not if things go bad: then brave or stupid is both dead, and it don't matter. No, but when it turns out good, the brave person feels better about herself having done the right thing, whereas the stupid person knows deep down not only does she deserve no credit, but that someday, somewhere, she's gonna be just as stupid again.

I lay down and try to think of one good thing about all this. I fall asleep instead. I spend the next few days avoiding Maurice and trying to think of one good thing. It helps pass the time till we arrive at the planet nobody can pronounce, so why don't they just call it something easy. Right now it sounds like a Bronx Cheer, and I refuse to begin diplomatic relations by sticking my tongue between my lips and blowing a raspberry at these aliens.

I've had pictures to look at to prepare me for the first meeting, so I know they look like blobs of Silly Putty, shiny and gray-pink. Still it's weird when I see them for real because this Silly Putty is alive. They constantly stretch and wobble, looking like Casper the Friendly Ghost after he's gone through a cotton candy machine. Who can take them serious?

Now I am glad Maurice warned me, because on top of looking cute as cartoons, they come across so polite and sensitive, it could fool you if you hadn't grown up with Alice and didn't know someone could be all soft and gooshy outside and still be a bitch of steel on the inside. This thought gives me an idea. I imagine I'm home and these Unpronounceable Blobs are my family. Oh, sure, they act like they love you, but let them find out you're happy about something and they have to ruin it for you.

Like Ma's cousin Carmella. She coulda had her pick of the neighborhood boys, but she had to go and seduce the parish priest, which meant he's got to give up his church and marry her. Ruining his dreams wasn't enough for her. She proceeded to raise six Mafiosi sons. Make no mistake why nice Italian boys invented the Mob: their mothers.

You're probably thinking I'm too easy on the men just because I can always find an excuse for a guy and fall in love with him no matter how low his IQ or how cruel he treats a girl. You're absolutely right. This is why, not only will I imagine the Blobs is my family, but I will remember they are the enemy by seeing them as female Bellicosa-Delancys. The aliens won't know the difference, seeing as how they got no sex of their own, and I will remain immune to those deadly social pathogens, empathy and sympathy.

So, like Eve before me, I start naming. My main contact I talk to, I'm calling her Mizi, after my Aunt Mizi, both of them being blobby masses of gelatinous flesh without a clue of how disgusting they look.

This Mizi has anywhere from one to seven arm-things depending on her mood, and no face anyplace. The face thing bothers me cuz I keep talking to where the mouth is and she keeps turning away and I am not in the mood to dance. After a couple of do-si-dos, I say, "Hey! This is making me crazy. I did not come here across the interstellar void to cha-cha. Where's your face, for Chrissake?"

Okay, not so diplomatic, you're thinking, but remember, all your diplomats didn't do so well, neither. This Blob, she makes what sounds like a fart and tells me that her people talk with the mouth part facing away.

So I naturally point out it's genetic incompetence to put the mouth where you can't see it to talk to it and not to expect me to do that. Mizi gets this funny stillness, and I think I'm gonna be invited to leave right then, a new record.

Then she says—get this—they don't use their mouth to talk to each other, they use gestures. The sound-talking is something they copied from us, dontcha know, because they figured out it was how we humans communicate.

Score. Not one of those diplomat-anthropologist-military-jerks found that out. Jersey girl earns her ticket. Then I get to thinking—a mistake, but my blood sugar is low—and once I think something I have to say it. So I ask, if the mouth's not for talking but just for eating, how is it they can make sounds with it at all? Not to mention putting it on the back means you can't see what's going inside when you eat. Your cousin could substitute a worm for some linguine and you wouldn't know till you were chewing, and that's a bit late if you ask me.

Mizi starts with the farting noises again and begging my forgiveness. I say not to worry, no bad smell, and in some cultures on Earth farting is like a thank you after a good meal. I say this in part because I am supposed to be a diplomat after all, and in part, actually mostly, because we are going on six hours without a meal so I'm getting hungry and hinting, alright?

Mizi explains they don't eat with their mouths, neither. So naturally I ask, though I'm starting not to care about anything except maybe a pizza with black olives and onions, what the heck she's got a mouth for then, and—get this—she tells me it's not a mouth at all. It's an anus, and it's the only body part they have that can make the sounds of our language.

So I start laughing. No wonder they think humans are crazy, sticking our butts at their butts and "farting" ideas. I explain that humans eat and breathe here—and I point to my mouth—and we eliminate waste and pass gas through another hole at the other end. And just to make my point I let fly with a small but fruity one.

Well, she gets all excited, I mean, all seven arm thingies are out and waving. And she asks, "Two holes?"

I say, "Yes, two." I know what you're thinking, but I am not mentioning no other hole to her. Instead, I change the subject. "So what about a face?" I ask. "I need to know where to look when I talk."

She does some shifty thing with her skin, enough to give me a location that would put me facing her about right. Her "face" looks a lot like Teddy Roosevelt on Mount Rushmore, but I let it go for now. Mizi, the real one, she has a mustache, too.

Now that we got the talking and the face thing straightened out, I tell them if they want to hear me fart my appreciation back at them, they have to feed me first. Which they do, though it isn't until I'm alone in my room that I manage anything to write home about. Just for fun I try to fart the name of the planet, and it sounds about right.

So you're probably figuring we'll get chummy after solving the big butt-hole problem. Not this girl. Any fool can make friends with fart jokes. That don't mean you got me eating beans out of your hand.

In the morning, a knock at the door doesn't make me happy. Jet lag is to how I feel the way a headache is to death by a car bomb. Still, I am a diplomat these days, envoy of the planet Earth, so I crawl out of bed. When Mizi comes in, I even talk to her.

"Hey, fart-face!" I say, just pretending, you know, to be falling for the friends thing. "I feel like you look. My bones are all jelly, and my face is falling off. It might almost be worth dying just so's I could get off this rock and go back to Earth."

Mizi, she starts wiggling all her arms around, making me dizzy. "I'm making conversation and all you can do is shake like a bad disaster movie. You do your St. Vitus routine while I take a whiz. All that bouncing's making my bladder hurt."

Well, suddenly her whole body collapses on the ground, the individual arms kind of melt back in and she turns into a single blob of quivering jelly. Okay, so maybe rudeness kills them, I'm thinking. I experiment.

"Get some dignity about yourself. Am I the Ambassador of Earth or am I the Avon Lady trying to sell you a lot of bad perfume just because it's in a cute bottle?"

I turn my back on her road-kill impersonation and go into the bathroom thinking about my Aunt Celeste who collects Avon bottles. Says they'll be worth something someday, says she's gonna pass 'em on to her kids. I can just see Vito when he finds he can't get one penny at the pawn shop for them. He'll want to kill his mother, but she'll already be dead. Such is life on Earth. Here on Unpronounceable, I come out of the bathroom and Mizi is still wiggling, so I give up on her and decide to find breakfast on my own.

I head toward the room where I ate dinner the night before, hoping breakfast with strong coffee and lots of sugary, fatty carbohydrates is a concept at least one of the previous missionaries got across to the natives. Mizi, she kind of flops and oozes after me like a balloon filled with jumping beans.

I run slam into another Blob going around a corner. It's not as repulsive as you'd think. They're warm and soft, but not slimy. Like a giant hot water bottle. This gal I bump into, she's a real tank like my great-gramma Ronnie was. She takes

9

one look at Mizi and oop!, Mizi is on her feet and practically saluting. I feel a bit bad for Mizi, and so I go on the attack.

"Hey, you, how about a few interplanetary niceties like showing me a face, so's I can ream you for running me over."

Seven arms just shoot straight out of the tank-Blob and pop back in. Mizi starts to melt again, but manages to say, "Rose Delancy, Envoy of Earth, may I introduce [another-goddam-unpronounceable-name], high priest and doctor of Medicine."

I offer my hand, the Blob puts out a paw, and we shake. I let her know, "I can't pronounce your names and I'm not gonna waste time trying to provide comic relief for your otherwise empty lives. Forget it. You, I'm calling Ronnie, after my mother's grandmother."

"I'm honored."

"Don't be. She was mean and stubborn, and the Earth became a cheerier place the day she died." They both start up now. "Wiggle, wiggle, wiggle. What is with you people? Every time I open my mouth, you turn into tapioca. It's disgusting. Stop it."

More wiggling. "Hey. You may be talking in signs here, but I'm not hearing anything so I don't know what's going on."

"Our apologies. We are laughing. I keep forgetting, you humans make a screeching sound when you are happy. We will accommodate." And suddenly I'm in the middle of a slasher movie. Alfred Hitchcock, you lived in the wrong century. I start flailing my arms trying to get them to stop, and they just scream louder. I realize they think I'm trying to laugh in their language, and it's making things even funnier.

This pisses me off so I stop and stand absolutely still a few minutes, and the slaughterhouse soundtrack disappears. I am emphatic, "Don't do that ever again. You bozos can just wiggle from now on, and I'll know what it means."

"We were not correct in our replication of laughter?"

"You were correct, alright, but it was a replication from Hell."

"Hell is where, in your religion, souls go after life?"

"Only souls who do unspeakable evil and are tortured for all eternity, screaming and writhing in agony without end."

"Odd. That is the sound several of your predecessors made when they enjoyed a rejuvenation bath at a [*spitting-choking-word*]."

"They were screaming in pain, numbskull. You stripped off all their skin, which is not a thing that should ever be done to a person, or even to meat if it's still alive." Mizi and Ronnie become still and change color. I'm philosophical. "Hey, not to worry. Those losers were nuts to come here in the first place. No harm done."

Mizi and Ronnie brighten right up. "We did mean well. A [*spitting-choking-word*] for us is the highest experience of what it is to be an [Unpronounceable]. We were going to invite you tomorrow."

"And while I was screaming in pain, you sadists would have just wiggled with glee. You're a great bunch of gals, and if you don't feed me some breakfast right now, I'm gonna tell the whole planet Earth you did it on purpose and they should nuke you till you glow."

We go to the dining room and get some food. I sit on a chair. The gals don't sit exactly. Their legs just squish under them. Ronnie holds forth while I chow down.

"It's such a relief to know humans are capable of being properly concerned over bodily functions. Your predecessors never asked for food or sleep or would admit to elimination. Obviously, they were perverts sent off-world because their lives had no value to society. We tried to help them as a sign of interplanetary goodwill, but we kept failing. This is why we finally requested a sane person. You, we can talk to, and there is hope for peace between our people."

Now a diplomat would have clasped their hands and made some promise of friendship. Me, all I can say is, "Don't count on it. Humans wouldn't know peace if every last one of them was dead. This soup stuff needs salt."

Lots of laughter. I think they like me, and this does not bode well. If they think at all like me, war with the rest of

Earth is inevitable. These Blobs, they got no weapons, no ships; they're the ideal Evil Empire. The troops are probably already massing back home for the attack, and me, I would be your sacrificial lamb. Well, I have never been anybody's lamb, let me tell you. With a good lie, maybe faking an allergy to Blobs, I can go back tomorrow on the ship that brought me. They can blow up the place just as good without me.

Now before you get all indignant calling me a coward, remember, I'm just a gal from New Jersey. I could no more save a planet from the consequences of global incompatibility than I could keep my mouth shut at the dinner table. I'm scared, I run.

I finish eating and go hunt up Maurice, who is sweet on me and ripe to be conned into breaking a few rules. "Maurice, you gotta help me..."

He cuts me off. "I'm sorry Rose. I have strict orders. No matter how much you beg, I can't take you back to Earth." Something about the way he says it, I can see he hopes I'll beg anyway. I realize napalm couldn't be as bad as owing this guy a favor for the long three days we'd be together in that sardine-can size spaceship. Besides, I have never in my life admitted anyone was right about me when they were actually right.

"Don't flatter yourself. I gotta report to Earth, that's all, and you got the radio."

He huffs back at me, "Use the one in your office." I remind myself he's just some space-age oar-puller, shrug, and walk away like I know where I'm going. I look confident, that's what counts.

"Hey, Rose. You're going the wrong way." He's smirking.

"Are you sure?"

He nods. "Your office in your house, and your house..."

"I know where my house is. I just got turned around. Two things I always forget not to trust: my sense of direction and men." I do love getting the last word.

I phone back to Earth and spill all the dirt on the Blobs. My boss, a German guy named Reiner Something, his last name being another kind of spitting-choking-word I can't pronounce, he listens like he's heard it all before, which I know he hasn't. This makes me mad, because you can bet your diplomatic immunity that when he writes it up for the press, he's gonna make it sound like he figured it out on his own.

I'm all ready to say, "Listen, I've done what all your experts couldn't. Now that you know why they took your guys for crazy, and how come that skin problem happened, you can coach a real diplomat on the finer points of Blob-talk. You don't need me. I feel it's time to come home..." when, dontcha know, he interrupts me before I can say one word.

"Congratulations Rose, you've done what our experts couldn't. Now that we know why they thought our envoys crazy, and how come the [*spitting-choking-word*] problem happened, we can coach a real diplomat to take your place. You've served your purpose and it's time you came home."

This is a low blow. Although I really do want to go home, there's no way I'm leaving after that crack. "You wouldn't know a real diplomat if one told you with a straight face your personality has nothing to do with why people vomit every time they talk to you." Reiner gets mad, which don't surprise me, since I have that talent. Alice got perfect pitch. I got perfect aim.

Apparently Mizi and Ronnie came in and heard my last comment. I don't see them behind me, but Reiner does. He quick puts on a shmooze face and talks to them like I'm not even there.

"Your Excellencies, I am relieved that our misunderstandings in communication have been clarified. This will open the door to much more effective relations between our peoples, which I feel..."

I turn to Ronnie and interrupt Reiner by saying, "He's the switchboard operator, but he thinks he runs the United Nations. Humor him or he gets violent, but don't believe a thing he says."

"Is everyone in your government insane?"

"Of course. Who else would want to bother?"

"Isn't anyone in charge?"

"No, I don't think so."

Ronnie turns to Reiner, who is in fact the head of the United Nations. "Mr. Lichtendorfman, we are most happy with the current envoy, Rose Delancy. Please allow us to extend our invitation to her for an indefinite period of time. We have found her a most congenial ambassador and excellent communicator. We regret past errors, and for this reason we wish to limit human contact until we have been able to learn more of your race, and you of ours, so that in the future such mishaps can be avoided." Ronnie turns to me and whispers, "Can I handle crazies, or what?"

For the first time in weeks, I crack a smile. Reiner gets apoplectic, but what can he do? Earth is stuck with me being First Interplanetary Ambassador to the Unpronounceable Planet of Blobs for as long as I want the job.

Hey, Alice, I would call that going places, wouldn't you?

Chapter 2
Alien Sex

I am bored. I know, I know, I am on an uncharted alien world. So much to see, so much to do. But think about it. It's alien, which means nothing is familiar and so who cares? You seen one night sky with three moons, you're done. Moons don't mean nothing until you spend a couple hours looking up at one over Jimmy Petrankis' shoulder as he's huffing away in the back seat of his dad's convertible. After that, the moon, the steady thump of rock and roll music, the squeak of a Chevy suspension in need of a lube job, these take on meaning. A girl needs experiences before she can care.

At home, if the experiences weren't good, at least they kept me from being bored. I could fight with my family, and the time would pass. I could have sex with an inappropriate but good-looking man and forget who I was for a half-hour. And when all else failed, I could shop for things I couldn't afford and then fend off irate creditors for months, pretending not to speak English when they called. But notice, my family does not happen to reside in this particular solar system. There are no men, no creditors, no stores even. I tell you, I'm depressed, and it ain't pretty. I stopped dressing since nobody else wears clothes or even cares, stopped wearing make-up since faces are optional here as well, and finally went so far as to stop shaving my pits and legs.

Now, before anybody gets all grossed out, I should add that this particular slump in personal hygiene led to yet another interplanetary breakthrough. See, Mizi asked me about the leg stubble once, and I explained about shaving and how it was a mark of civilization, just one more boat she and her kind had missed. She did a little wobble, said she'd adjust the water, and walked away.

I'm so mesmerized watching her rolling backside disappear around the corner I don't really think about what she said. But dontcha know, the next day when I shower, not only does my stubble wash away, but all of my hair falls out. Everywhere. Needless to say, I am not happy, but needless doesn't stop this girl. I say plenty, drawing a bit of a crowd as I'm wishing loudly for an axe, explaining I want to show them a typical human type called an "axe murderer," and dontcha know, the Blobs go and bring me one. Can you beat that? I get even madder, saying how, by giving me an actual axe, they cheat me not only of the fun of using it, because an ambassador can't commit dismemberment on anyone, but also of the sweet dream that I would if I could.

Mizi says, no, no, be her guest, and invites me to haul off and whack her with it right on her sort-of head. Maybe you'd be ashamed to vent on someone who's being so agreeable, but not me. I whack. And then I bounce. The axe not only doesn't hurt Mizi, it ricochets back so quick I'm off balance and falling on my behind quicker than you can say Lizzie Borden.

"Mizi," I explain, "I did not want the axe so's I could practice for a vaudeville comedy act. I wanted it so I could split your head open and watch your precious bodily fluids ooze out onto the floor. Then I figured we'd be even."

Mizi says okay and invites me to try again. Now I hesitate. See, if this was Alice or anybody else from my family, it would be a set up. I'd trust, whack, and fall right back on my behind again, and they'd all laugh for days.

I decide to go ahead as a kind of test. If she's playing me for the goat, I'll know all this friendship baloney is just a set-up for the takeover of planet Earth, and I can always have the last laugh by giving the Blobs a nuclear winter to remember.

I swing the axe one more time and bring it down hard on Mizi's noggin-equivalent. It hits with a solid thunk. The pink-grey flesh splits, leaving a huge gash, out of which oozes all manner of slimy innards and buckets of blood. Mizi collapses on the ground and wiggles in convulsive throes, sending splats of soft grayish effluvia everywhere. I do my part and throw up.

The other Blobs are watching, and it occurs to me I will have a hard time explaining this when Reiner asks why I have been kicked off the planet. Then suddenly all the many-colored and many-textured parts of Mizi just ooze back together and there she is, back in her normal disgusting shape. The only mess left is the bits of my lunch that I lost. Those cookies stay put where I tossed them.

"How was that?" Mizi is obviously pleased with her performance, and the other Blobs are crowding around impressed. So am I, not that I'd show it.

"Thanks for making me throw up. Now I get to eat another tasteless, texture-less lunch. But first, I gotta brush my teeth. They won't fall out like my hair did, will they?"

The Blobs give a smile of a wiggle and assure me my teeth are safe. And Mizi promises to adjust the water back to normal and just give me a special washcloth that will do the same trick, but only in the places I rub it. They also will rig a cloth to hurry the growth of hair back on my head. So I'm only bald for a couple of days. In a week, I have a nice head of curls. Not only that, my hair is silkier and shinier than it ever was in my life.

A more business-savvy girl might be wondering how a world that doesn't have a single factory has managed to produce these nifty hair and skin care products. Beauty products have always been a sure way to get rich back home, and most of those don't actually do much more for your skin than good old olive oil does. Beauty products that actually improve your skin and hair would make so much money, rich would seem poor by comparison. Me, though, all I can think about is Mizi's special-effects performance.

After a few days, so she won't think I'm at all impressed, just bringing it up for polite chit-chat, I ask, "So how'd you do that blood-and-guts trick the other day?"

"Oh, that's nothing. We can take any form we like."

"Do you mean to say you choose to have that shapeless body in that ugly color?"

"Appearance is irrelevant."

"It may not bother you, but think about someone else for a minute, like me, for instance. I'm the one stuck with sensory deprivation, looking at nothing but Blobs all day, eating tasteless food, and having sex all by myself."

"Looks are so important to you humans perhaps because you cannot change them."

"Not without a pile of cash and a top-notch plastic surgeon."

"Would you be happier if I looked like you?" Mizi shifts before my eyes and becomes the spitting-image of me.

"Gah! No, no. I'm the last person I'd want to be marooned on a distant planet with. No one should have to be stuck with herself. No. Give me Mad Max. James Bond. Indiana Jones. All the movie idol guys."

"Your government showed us some movies. I started to watch one, got bored, and left."

"We'll watch together and I'll explain. For one thing, the guys, look at the guys. Chiseled jaw, rippling chest, biceps to die for, and hair always in the right place. Just the sight of one tells you God's in his heaven and all's right with the world. Whereas the sight of you makes me think God got a phone call from his mother right in the middle of creation, and he had to drop everything unfinished and hurry over because her cat was on the roof and wouldn't come down."

Mizi, still looking like me, takes off all of a sudden and I figure she's mad. No that I care. I've made people mad all my life, and I'm not gonna stop now. It's weird, though, seeing yourself walk away in a huff.

I flop down on my sofa and sigh. I should be happy. I'm the first Interplanetary Ambassador to the Unpronounceable Planet of the Blobs, for Chrissake. I'm living in a palace, sitting in a salon that could entertain the rich and famous and make them swoon. Huge rooms, vaulted ceilings, comfortable arty-farty furniture. Even the food, tasteless though it is, you can tell it's healthy, you know, like the kind your vegan friends serve, swearing it's just as good as mom used to make, which makes you think if this is how their mom used to cook, no wonder they have a sick relationship with food.

My Ma was a gourmet cook. The only time I ever saw her pick up canned soup or sauce was when she'd use it to nail a teenager about to commit mayhem two rooms away. She'd been a champion at stoop ball in her youth, and she never lost her aim. She kept the cans my father's family sometimes brought over so's she'd have something to practice with, but anything that went on our table to actually eat was made from scratch. If Uncle Johnny hadn't lied about having put the fish pate for Cousin Gina's wedding in the fridge, she'd still be making tortellini today. Of course, in the inscrutable logic of Italian culture, Uncle Johnny was absolved, lie and all, and my Ma was blamed for her own demise for having entrusted food to a man in the first place.

This could scar any eleven-year-old, such as I was at the time. Add to that the approach of puberty. And the fact that Ma was the only person on the planet Alice couldn't fool who loved her anyway—me being the only other person she couldn't fool, but love went down the toilet with my second pet fish. Ma had bought me the fish after the carnival fish died and I was all broke up about it. One day, I noticed Goldie wasn't eating her food. A couple days later, she was floating at the top of the tank. Alice shrieked like the dead fish grossed her out, grabbed the bowl, dumped the contents in the toilet, and flushed before I even knew what was happening.

Anyway, I decide enough moping alone in my room. I'll go find Mizi and make up, even though I'm not sure she's even mad. See how noble being an ambassador can make you. Only as I'm going out, in walks Mad Max himself in full post-apocalyptic leather. He looks at me and smiles that wet-your-pants smile and says in Mizi's voice, "How's this?"

I must say I'm impressed. And irritated. "The voice ruins it."

"Is this better?" She sounds just like him. This could be interesting.

"Okay. Tell me how beautiful I am."

"Rose, you are the most beautiful girl on the planet." He says this with a wicked grin, for I am also the only girl on the planet.

I chuck a thing like a vase of flowers at him. He ducks. The vase, as well as the flowers, smash to bits, and nobody cares. What will happen to the broke vase and stuff, I couldn't say, but it'll be gone in an hour and a new one will appear sooner or later. Go figure. Me, I'm contemplating a pair of green eyes and trying not lose my head. This is only Mizi after all, even if the mouth that's talking is Mad Max all the way.

"Rose, I'd think you were beautiful even if you weren't the only girl on the planet. I'm a Blob, after all. I think shapeless flesh is the ideal." More grinning.

I'm losing, okay. A beautiful hunk of a guy with a sense of humor after my own heart could do anything he wanted with me. I take a step closer and notice the clothes are not something he's wearing. They are part of him. This will not do, but the guy-disguise has affected my hormonal balance enough to make me point out gently, "It's a sweet trick. But you are the clothes, too. That's weird."

"It's just an experiment. I can get clothes and make it more human."

"How did you do it?"

"I called up your government and asked them to show me a scene from one of those movies you mentioned. What does this face mean?" Mizi immediately shifts features. She not only copies perfectly a weirded-out eyebrows-raised expression of astonishment, she actually does it with the face of the person himself. Pretty neat.

"That expression means he thinks you're insane."

The face shifts back to Max, and we both laugh. I have a sudden thought and put my hand on his crotch. Sure enough, he could have been a Ken doll. I remind myself this is just an alien Blob that only looks like a hormonally perfect-to-be-father-of-my-children kind of guy. Still, if the Blobs is good at copying...

"If you're gonna make the clothes optional, you gotta get the rest of you anatomically correct. We're gonna need some things—an anatomy book with pictures. Fashion magazines, so everybody else here can look good, too."

A thought crosses my mind, and the unfamiliarity of such a thing makes me panic. If everyone else here looks like a fashion plate, I'll be back to plain Jane. "And then I'll be the only ugly one on a planet of beautiful people. I hate you, and if you don't leave now, I'll hold my breath until I die." I grab a big lungful of air and hold it while Max/Mizi throws his/her arms out in a gesture even I can recognize as frustration, and leaves. I decide to do penance by cleaning up the vase, but it is already gone, so I go to sleep even though it's still daylight outside.

Somewhere in the middle of the night, there's a pounding on my door and somebody's screaming, "Stella! Stella!" I'm dreaming I'm back home, I guess, but I go along with it, getting up to tell the jerk to pipe down or I'll call the cops. Marlon Brando in a t-shirt barges in, picks me up, throws me on the bed, and lays his body on top of me. I realize something's not quite right for this to be reality, but I don't think it's a dream either. Then I realize this is not the body of a large lusting man; this is Mizi in another disguise. I am frustrated, and this brings back my natural belligerence.

"First of all, you are the wrong color." I explain about black-and-white film. Mizi colorizes Stanley before my eyes.

"You also smell wrong. No wonder you people have no culture. No looks to teach you beauty, no smells to mark one thing from another... I mean, what's the point if you're just a Blob?"

"It is humans who do not have interesting bodies, as far as we can tell." Oho. The gloves are off. The true nature of these Blobs is coming out. They are obnoxious.

"We manage to pick a shape, hold it, and use it as a UNIQUE tool for life. You can't keep one shape long enough to take a picture and send it home to mother."

"Why would I want a picture? No one cares what I look like."

"That's why you're a shallow, boring people with no art worth looking at, no food worth eating, and no objects to covet so a girl can go shopping and take her mind off men."

"Why does it always come back to men?"

"Because of the whole reason Stanley calls to Stella. Because of what he did next with the thing he has here." I put my hand on Mizi's crotch for emphasis, and dontcha know, this time there was something there. Something plenty. "Oh, this. You got one."

"I read an anatomy book."

"Yeah, well there's more to it than pictures can tell."

"I also watched films. This part grows like so," —and did it ever— "and then the man and the woman do this." His clothes, which had been just part of him shifted to bare skin. Young Marlon Brando naked. I could get used to this.

"You still smell wrong."

"Picky, picky. How about this?"

"Uh-uh. Old guy."

"The first Ambassador."

"Try the French one." I am assaulted by loud cologne. I sneeze. "Bad idea."

"How about this?" It is Maurice. Right down to the breath mint. I am about to object about copying the smell of somebody I actually know and then figure what he don't know won't hurt him. Plus, it's a kind of revenge. I like it, in fact.

"Oh, what the hell."

You know, having sex with an alien who can control length, and width, and texture—yes even texture, girls—is not half bad. I'm starting to like it here. But I'm not telling anybody back home about the extraterrestrial extracurriculars.

Chapter 3
Trick or Treaty

Alien sex may be fun, but I am still the Ambassador from Earth with a job to do. Only nobody really explained the job to me, seeing as how they expected me to fail like the proverbial 10-day miracle diet. To be honest, so did I.

Now I'm learning on the job, trying to figure out what an Ambassador does besides screw with the natives. I phone back to Earth, and Reiner Whatsisname tells me not to worry about the job, that just by being here, I'm doing it. And doing just fine, they couldn't be more pleased. He says this with such an air of warm encouragement that I know the powers-that-be are up to something and it isn't nice. He smiles like Alice does when she's about to tell you that your new boyfriend, he's gonna take her to the movies instead.

I check with Mizi who is at present going through a Cary Grant phase, don't matter which movie, he always looks the same, kind of like the Blobs only pretty, holding out a box of chocolates, a bouquet of flowers, and an unspeakably attractive smirk. I get a momentary flutter and then remember this guy is only Silly Putty dressed up to look like an evolutionary masterpiece. Makes it easier to stick to business.

"Hey Pinkie. Does this planet have anything valuable like oil, or minerals, or...stuff?"

"We could. What do you want?"

"No, no. Not stuff you could make. Stuff Nature makes. Like gold or uranium..."

"All that is possible. The planet is very responsive."

"You mean, if you need something, the planet makes it for you?"

"Of course. And you can have as much as you want."

"Don't say that in earshot of any real estate developer or mining consortium, or pretty soon it'll be just like Earth here, and I'd have to find a new planet with intelligent life to screw around on."

"Don't go, Rose."

"Okay, but only if you tell everybody else to stay away until I say so."

Then I sniff the flowers absentmindedly, having never been given two dozen long-stem red roses before, only to find they smell like old socks. I drop them on the floor by way of Cary's head.

While he ducks, I am opening the chocolates, figuring to drown my sorrows in a few thousand calories of sweet self-indulgence. I'm missing candy so much, I don't even choose a caramel, chocolate-covered caramels being the one food that if I ate as much as I truly wanted, it would send me into insulin shock and a quick but sated death. I rip the top off the box, grab a lump, and bite. Sewage. After I finish gagging, I call the aforementioned Blob-in-screen-idol's-clothing every bad word I learned that summer at camp from Lena Kolzitski, the Slavs really having mastered the art of invective.

Cary, aka Mizi the Blob, keeps saying he didn't know they were for eating and that he tried to stop me, and how could he possibly know what chocolate tastes like since he hadn't never had any. The Blobs can't make a taste they don't know, after all. This shuts me up as I realize the reason everything here is so tasteless is that it is based on the tasteless crap that passes for spaceship food, which is just like airplane food, only older.

So duh, I just figured out my job as the ambassador to this godforsaken planet. They can make anything look like anything, you know, pretty and shiny and sexy, but empty. No taste. No smell. No junk food. Me, I'm gonna bring culture to these natives, if it kills them.

For example, the Cary Grant standing in front of me all suave in a suit needs to smell like booze. High class booze, not your box wine or nothing, but maybe scotch on the rocks or at least bathtub gin. After a month of nonstop sex, Maurice and his breath mint are getting stale. It was fine when we was making our way through all the dirtball scumbags of the silver screen, but it don't go with high class sex toys like Cary here.

"Something's missing. The sex is entertaining, but there's more to life."

"Like what?"

"Hell if I know."

So we have sex. Cary Grant is maybe not as ripped as your modern movie star, but he was a dancer, dontcha know, so he moves like a cat and bends like, well, a Blob, yes I know it's just pretend, but who can remember at times like this when the man is just perfect.

The next morning, naturally I'm sleeping in, when wouldn't you know the communication center sirens go off. Somebody from Earth wants to talk to me. Oh, goody.

I grope without opening my eyes all the way and manage to push the right button. A well-groomed woman clearly in need of adding prunes to her diet tells me to hold for the President of the United States. Can you beat that? Calls me, wakes me up in fact, and then has the nerve to ask me to hold. I hang up.

A minute and it's ringing again, but by this time I have found some clothes and am ready for them. Even I know better than to talk to the President while topless. You don't get the right kind of respect.

"Hello Rose. Let me congratulate you on behalf of all Americans on the honor of having one of our own selected to be the Ambassador to the..." and here the dope tries to pronounce it. He don't even come close, but I don't laugh. See, I was laughed at once for my pronunciation of the French word, voilà—I said it like boiler. Apparently that was wrong. Now, I refuse to try even your basic Earthwise foreign languages, let alone any extraterrestrial ones. The Pres, he should do likewise.

But I don't tell him direct. I say, "The Blobs are alright."

"Blobs?"

"Who can say their name without sounding like a moron with a cleft palate? Not me. Not you." See how diplomatic I hint? "Blobs describes them, and they like it."

"'Blobs' is not very flattering."

"Yeah, well you should see the gesture they make for humans." I execute a fine male masturbation shake of the wrist and see the President blush. I neglect to add that I taught them the gesture. First rule of diplomacy, don't say too much.

"Rose, the United States has a big request to make of you. You love your country, don't you?"

Do I tell the President I couldn't love a place that was stupid enough to elect him? Okay, so they never proved the graft, but the massacre and pillage of dissidents in a minor South American dictator's democratic stronghold was there for everybody to see. Fortunately for him, Americans actually believe a person who waves the flag while getting rich robbing foreigners and political losers when he whines that he has just been given a raw deal by the press. Me, I buried the family silver the day he took office. So I huff and puff and beg the question, "What a thing to ask a girl from New Jersey!"

"Rose, you misunderstand. I don't doubt you for a minute. No, it's just some people think that we are all, oh, one world, something like that, and don't think their country should come first."

"Hey, like I tell every guy I date, I come first or I fix it so's he never comes again."

"That's exactly what I'm hoping you'll arrange with the... er...Blobs."

"What? My country wants me to come with one of them? Alien sex! Me, a good Catholic girl from the Garden State? "

"Good heavens, no. I meant..."

"But since you brought up the sex thing, I have to tell you, the Blobs are really very curious about it, seeing as they have no sex of their own. So, in the interest of education only, I'm thinking the next shipment should include some serious porn vids."

"Rose, I don't think that's, well, the America we want them to know."

"Maybe you're right. Send some French porn. We'll only give them the best of America—the food. Let me see. You got a pencil? Hot dogs with all the fixings and some board-walk fries. Burgers, too. Oh, and Velveeta and Wonder Bread. And pizza, New York Style, naturally. Cheesecake, too. With beer, Milwaukee beer, that's what I want. For them to experi-ence. Jack Daniels also, cases of it."

"Rose, I find it hard to believe the Blobs want Jack Daniels."

"They want to try everything. I just figured we'd give 'em the all-American experience first. You know, Whitman Sam-pler, Ritz Crackers, and Frosted Flakes. And peanut butter. God, I almost forgot peanut butter. Grape jelly is the classic second, but let us not forget bacon and bananas. Ice cream is also good, preferably rocky road. And, of course, apple pie."

"It is too expensive to send something as trivial as real food into space."

"Trivial! The Blobs have a saying; 'you are what you eat.' They mean it quite literally. They keep saying how we can't be civilized on account we got no taste. See, they only have tasted that freeze-dried space food, and well, that's what they think we are. Oh, also bubble gum. Ronnie will get a kick out of that, I'm sure."

"Miss Delancy…"

"What happened to 'Rose'?"

"Rose, we cannot accommodate your outrageous requests, which I suspect come not from the Blobs, as you call them, but for your own personal use and gratification."

"I am on a diet, I will have you know. Do you know how many calories there are in peanut butter? And rocky road, well, a girl might as well just spoon that stuff onto her hips. I'm not saying I won't eat any of it, but only to be polite and keep company while the Blobs sample, that's all. Besides, didn't you have a favor to ask?"

Suddenly I'm getting his biggest crocodile smile, the one he saves for religious fanatics and political extremists who will mortgage their home to elect a fraud who tells them the lies they love to hear. "Rose, I'll tell you how it is. You can have anything you want so long as you can get a military base for it."

"I do not remember mentioning military bases. The Blobs wouldn't be interested in those. They got no war. Never have."

"Not for the Blobs. For us. For America."

"Ah."

"That's what I called to ask you. See, Rose, the last President made some pretty stupid treaties about reducing weapons stockpiles, and the Congress ratified it, and well, here we are, stuck with having to get rid of some pretty expensive and powerful tools of national defense. And I thought, well, if the Blobs would just let us build a storage facility out in their countryside somewhere, we could just tuck those babies in nice and neat. The treaty inspection teams here on Earth could verify the weapons were indeed gone, and everybody could be happy."

"You want the Blobs to help you break the treaty?"

"We are not breaking the treaty. Absolutely not. America stands by its agreements. Our lawyers are clear in their interpretation that the weapons' absence of presence on the planet Earth will constitute compliance with the treaty. America gets to have its cake and eat it, too."

"What kind of cake are we talking, here?"

"What kind is your favorite, Rose?"

"Uh, that would be Devil's food."

"Consider it done. Now, about that treaty..."

"I'll check with the Blobs and get back to you. Meanwhile, if I was you, I'd sniff out what the United Nations is up to. They got something in the works, and it's a stinker, judging by how much perfumy language they're spraying around here."

"That Lichtendorfman!" —the Pres should not say that name either— "He'd stab you in the back if he thought you were in his way. Don't trust a word he says, Rose."

"Right, Chief." And we hang up all chummy.

I know, I know. Now you all hate me, right. Half of you are thinking alien miscegenation. Time to burn some crosses on that girl's front lawn. If only pick-up trucks could cross the interstellar void. The rest of you are thinking imperialist invasion. First the missiles, then the Twinkies and music videos, and pretty soon Unpronounceable becomes just another dispirited colonized people.

First of all, they ain't people, they're Blobs. Second, you may have started thinking the Blobs are all sweet and gooshy because they're catering to my every whim, no questions asked. Now seriously, do you buy that? Me neither. They are up to something, just as sure as Reiner and the Pres. As a matter of fact, the only person who ain't up to nothing in this whole mess is me. I'm just the boob everybody's hoping to play for the patsy. It's time for that to change.

I grab the micro-vid camera and set it up with a clear view of the bed. Mizi, à la Cary Grant in the nude, is still asleep as I go undercover. Pretty soon he's awake and back to pleasing Rose, which means life is full of new and surprising sensations, but I don't forget my mission. I let him do his best job of sucking up to Rose, and put on the performance of my life pretending I'm enjoying myself. Okay, so that part wasn't so hard.

After we've explored just about every angle of the problem of pleasing Rose, I excuse myself to go pee, tucking the video chip away, safe in my box of tampons. When I return, he's awake and I'm ready for battle.

"So, Mizi. How come you're so nice to me when you don't get nothing out of it? I mean, the sex is just a picture show in 3-D for you."

"I like you, Rose."

"Oh, sure. And I like you, too. I like you so much I have been filming our little love nest activities here so's I can share them with the folks back home. Then I'm gonna tell them you're planning to body snatch every young virgin on the planet and force her to sodomize your multiple members. They'll vaporize this planet without a how-dee-do."

"What's 'sodomize?'"

"We'll get into that later. Right now I want the truth, the whole truth, and nothing but the truth. What are you up to? Spill."

Mizi goes all quivery, and let me tell you, Cary Grant waggling his ears, legs, arms, nose, and what-not is not a pretty sight. Mizi's giggling in Blob. I start laughing too.

Wiping away a tear, a nice effect I must say, he/she explains. "I told Ronnie we couldn't fool you. She said what's to lose? It's not like you could complain to those idiots who keep calling from Earth. Admit it. You like us more." Coming out of the face of Cary Grant with that conspiratorial wink, I feel my resolve start to slip. I tell you, if it wasn't for men, women would rule the world. I catch myself just in time.

"I refuse to have this conversation with a fictional movie star. Go back to your normal blob-ness so we can talk official interplanetary business."

Mizi, in her normal voice and face, starts explaining. "Rose, we want to send an emissary to Earth. I've been practicing with you so I can fit in and get along with humans."

"You boob! You can't practice on me. Learning what I like will teach you how to make most humans hate you. They may be stupid, but that don't mean they're not dangerous."

"But you're the only human we can stand. Everyone else we talk to on those interplanetary conference calls goes in circles about trade and defense, financial ties and sovereignty, property and privacy. Not a one of us can eat or sleep for hours after even a short conversation. Do you realize, I have personally spoken six or seven times with your UN Secretary General, and I still don't know what food he loves so much that if he could eat his fill, it would kill him?"

"Because, Pancake-Face, if he knew he could eat his fill, he wouldn't want it anymore. He'd want something else, something he couldn't have."

"So if he thinks he can't have "Unpronounceable"...

"He'll spend every last resource of the Earth to get it."

"Are we in trouble?"

"Yup."

"What do we do?"

I don't know what you do when the fate of a planet is at stake. I tell Mizi if we was getting screwed by Earth, we'd better practice some evil sex, so we switch to playing Ricardo Montalban as Khan making love to the sexy lieutenant on the deck of the Enterprise. Mizi gives Khan every inch of evil a girl could ask for, even though she don't have to any more, and so another day on Unpronounceable goes by without me having to get out of bed.

Next day though, me, Mizi, Ronnie, and a bunch of big-ass Blobs meet for a pow-wow. I open the proceedings with an eloquent tirade for the assembled dignitaries.

"Ladies and Unpronouceables, don't get me wrong. Personally I think this planet is an ugly lump of rock and wouldn't want my worst enemy to spend a week let alone a lifetime here. But I am not in charge of the policies of planet Earth. And considering the trouble everybody back there is taking over this cheerless backwater, you folks are in for the invasion of your lives. The question is not whether, but whether you will have any say about how, when, and by whom you will be taken over. I am not asking you to trust me..."

"Good thing." That's a gal named Gaudi heckling. She's so old she can hardly hold a shape, and her pink is all mottled with little chocolate-colored globs like somebody hot-glued Cocoa Crispies onto a water bottle. She reminds me of this truly weird cathedral in Spain I saw a picture of once. Gaudi was the name of the architect of that catastrophe.

"...for the same reason I don't waste my breath making deals with cockroaches. I don't see them, they can live like kings. Run across my kitchen floor when the light is on, and the heel of my shoe will grind them into the linoleum before the question of trust comes up for discussion."

I continue. "Assuming I got reasons of my own for wanting to keep you unappealing, overgrown, sentient pimples out of the itchy fingers of the separate or united nations of Earth, I have a couple of ideas that will at least buy us some time before the fleets descend and the fleecing starts."

A neon pink Blob chirps, "I have a hard time imagining such a thing could really happen," which just proves bright colors in a Blob don't mean bright ideas.

"Next time you talk to the Japanese, ask about Admiral Perry and see if I exaggerate. Meanwhile, you want I should spill my stall tactics or not?"

Ronnie sighs, "I'd rather take a nap, but alright."

Ronnie is sounding more and more like me, which has got to stop, but I don't mention it just now. Instead, I whip out my little surprise. It is a big rectangle of Blob-pink cloth with wavy white lines across like a TV in the old days that don't get a good signal and a blue circle in the middle like a big, fat zero. My design. Pink, white and blue. It came to me in a flash of inspiration while I was soaking in the tub, and I'm rather proud of it.

The Blobs, almost in a chorus, respond. "Ugly as last week's garbage." "Putrid. That's a word isn't it?" "Oh, yeah, putrid's a word, and that's the picture that goes with it." "Yuck. I feel sick. Can I go home now?"

You see why I love these gals.

"Pay attention. This is your flag. From now on, whenever you talk to Earth, make sure this or one like it is in the background and can be seen on the screen. This says that every scrap of land on the planet, even if it is a wasteland that no self-respecting Blob would be caught dead visiting, all of it, every grain of dirt, every drop of water is ours, ours, ours, and if you take any without permission, we will fight the good fight until every last one of you thieving thieves is dead."

"We could never say that."

"You don't say it. The flag does it for you. Neat, huh?"

They pass it around and all the Blobs who have palavered with Earth talk about all the different flags that are always behind the head of every head of state.

"Second stall technique: send an ambassador to begin negotiations for a treaty. Ronnie came up with half an idea that fooled me for about twenty minutes, namely to teach Mizi to get along with humans so she could go to Earth as an envoy and keep an eye on the natives. Right idea, wrong Blob. They'd never trust Mizi. To trust her, they'd have to believe she'd betray her people in the hope of being chums with humankind. Like me with you, only the reverse."

Gaudi again. "How do you know this isn't exactly the idea the humans on Earth came up with in sending you?"

I give her a withering look and turn to the Blob next to her. "Ronnie, you've talked with the UN people. Do you think they could come up with a plan like that?"

"Impossible."

"This is one of the deep psychoses of your human psyche. They got no problem believing one of you would throw over your whole planet for human civilization and enterprise while being rock solid on the impossibility of even the lowest human, in this case me, betraying noble humanity to blobby pink pustules such as yourselves."

"But that's insane."

"Exactly. Which is why you have to find me an insane Blob. One you gals can't stand because she's so twisted she lives without really enjoying it, loves her self-image more than reality, pretends to like everything she hates and hate everything she secretly likes, and wants everybody to be nice and at least act like they like her no matter what she does to them."

"You are describing the insane people your planet sent us to cure."

"They don't think they're insane on Earth. On Earth, those are the powerful, the rich, and the celebrated. They're what Earth thinks is the best."

"Where do you fit in, then?"

"They figured, if you didn't appreciate their best, they'd send their worst. Me."

We laughed a long time over that. Eventually I call the meeting back to order.

"These are just stalls. The treaty your nutcase comes up with, you don't have to sign it, or even read it. It just postpones the inevitable flattening you are about to experience under that steamroller called "Interspecies Friendship and Cooperation." Right now you got one human on your planet, and look how much trouble I am. Then remember, there are three to four billion just like me back on Earth."

A collective freeze goes through the room. They're so brittle with horror, one soprano hitting high C, and bam!, I'd be knee-deep in pinkish pebbles. Almost makes me wish Alice was here. She could do it, voice-wise, and malice-wise. But enough happy daydreams.

"This is why you need a scheme that will make every single government on Earth take a hands-off attitude toward Unpronounceable. This is where I come in."

Gaudi, she heckles again. "And to achieve that end, we just do everything you say."

I smile. "Give that gal a plastic key chain! The difference between me and them ain't the honor of our tactics, no, but that I admit every step of the way I'm doing it for selfish and self-gratifying reasons."

"But of course. Why else bother?"

"And as soon as I come up with the plan, I'll let you know. This meeting is adjourned. Let's eat something."

Chapter 4
Holy Swiss Cheese

So I get to make war on the human race with the resources of an entire planet at my disposal. Gives me goosebumps just saying it. Don't imagine I want to drop bombs and blow them to bits or nothing. That's only fun once, like a joke with a punch line. Sure you laugh the first time Uncle Roy tells it, but when he can't resist telling it again and again every time the family gets together, it makes Sister Hubert Mary's sex education class fascinating by comparison. Generals at war are basically Uncle Roy with stars on the shoulder; same punch line for five thousand years. Men have no imagination.

My idea of the perfect warrior is the Hollywood blonde with a major boob job, her D-cups riding shotgun as only silicon can, whom the sweaty money guys are drooling to cast just so's they can lose fortunes into her luscious cleavage, never mind the surgery makes them melons hard as coffee cans. Those losers actually believe this creamy amazon is attracted to them, paunch, bad breath, and hairy ears being the kind of thing a girl of twenty-two dreams of in a man of fifty. And all the while she's keeping notes, so that when her own turgid flesh starts to sag and they drop her flat, making jokes now about "the bimbo," she can go and publish, leaving several dead of apoplectic heart failure and the rest hiding from irate investors and indignant wives. She quietly restores the bazooms to mere boobs, and spends the rest of her days in the laugh of luxury with two large dogs and not a mogul in sight.

Phase one, Ronnie shows up in my office. She's bringing the gal I'd been told was the most maladjusted Unpronounceable they could find. Right away I can tell something is not-right with this Blob. She's practically solid; not a wobble disturbs the aerodynamic lines. I've been on Unpronounceable long enough so that her unchanging shape makes her look perverted, but in a bad way.

Mizi brings up the rear and shuts the door behind her.

"Hey, Ronnie. I see you've driven another innocent over the edge."

"Hello, Rose. I have been studying your history of electro-shock therapy. Is that what they did to you as a child?"

Ronnie and me, we are dangerously close to becoming pals. I am about to toss out another friendly insult, when this new Blob bows to me, can you believe it.

"You must be Rose, the emissary. I am so happy to meet you at last. It's been my dream to meet someone from your planet. I can tell just by looking at you that you are everything I hoped for and more."

"Really? Is it my bad breath or my cellulite that won you over."

"Ha, ha. You are so funny. That's just what everybody says. But no one mentioned what a lovely person you were on the inside. I'm very intuitive about these things. If I could just have a moment of your time in private, there are a few things your so-called friends have been doing that I think you should know about…"

Ronnie wraps a tentacle around what I guess to be the neck of our candidate and squeezes. She bulges above and below, looking now kind of like the Michelin Man, only pink. It don't look comfortable, and I'm thinking if this Blob has an ounce of sense, she will stop with the secrets and start over with the weather. Instead, she gets on her high horse.

"How dare you! What will humans think of us if we go around bullying each other? Shame on you. I think you owe

Ambassador Delancy an apology for acting in such an un-civilized manner in her office." And with that she gives the Blob-gesture equivalent of a smirk and actually sits in a chair like a human, only without arms and legs. Ronnie's tentacle has still not unwrapped, but now Our Blob of Perpetual Snit is ignoring it.

Mizi is loving this, rippling like the whole Rockettes line is dancing across her body. I'm smiling, too. "Hey, Ronnie, is that your kid you're strangling?"

"You wanted insane, you got it."

I may not be a psychiatrist, but I know how to poke around the ego with the best of them. I turn to Miss Snit, whom I have already begun thinking of as Alice. "So tell me, Alice, may I call you Alice?"

"My name is [the-sound-the-cat-made-when-cousin-Tony-ran-over-it-with-the-car]."

"Alice is the name of my sister, and everyone agrees she's the prettiest, smartest, and most talented member of our family."

"Alice would be alright, I guess."

"So, I was wondering how come you're so ugly."

Well, Alice gets positively brittle and looks from Ronnie to Mizi to me and back so fast I think she's gonna drill her-self right through the chair into the floor. "I can't believe you would stand by and let this, this…alien insult someone of my rank and character." She rises and starts to roll away in a pretty impressive huff. Unfortunately, Ronnie still has her by the sort-of-neck, and it kind of ruins the dramatic effect to get jerked back into her chair with a splat.

"Now, now, [sound-of-cat-getting-run-over]," Ronnie soothes. "She's an emissary from another world. We don't know their customs. She may have just complimented you, for all we know. She did give you her sister's name, after all. The rest of us are just aunts and cousins."

Mizi's belly's rippling around now like a frozen custard ma-chine spewing out a strawberry swirl. That don't stop her from pitching in for the cause. "We need you, Alice. Go and make a treaty for us with the people of Earth. You're our only hope."

You would not fall for it. I would not fall for it. Alice, however, says, "Wellll, okay. If you need me, I'll go, even though I hate the thought of being so far away from the home I love. Nevertheless, I'm willing to sacrifice it all for the common good. Can I leave today?" She tugs at her leash.

Ronnie still ain't letting go. "Can you be ready in an hour?"

"I'll have to say goodbye to all my friends."

"That'll take an extra five minutes."

"And family."

"Ten."

Mizi asks, "Don't you want a last [*spitting-choking-word*]?

"Don't disgust me." Alice turns to me. "Do they have a [*spitting-choking-word*] on Earth?"

"Not that I ever heard of."

"It sounds like paradise to me."

With that, Ronnie unhooks, and Alice flounces out, if a giant, semi-gelatinous pink blob can be said to flounce.

Ronnie turns to Mizi. "'Go and make a treaty with the people of Earth,'" she says and starts doing the custard ripple herself. "She couldn't negotiate her own bowel movement."

"Girls," I say. "While Alice is down on Earth making nice…" At the word "nice" both Mizi and Ronnie look like they're gonna be sick. I may not like these Blobs, but I do love them. "…we have to put a plan in action. And fast."

"Why the hurry, Rose?"

"Let me explain again, now that there's Alice to help me illustrate. I got no more clout with my people than Alice does with you, see. I don't like them any more than Alice likes you. I go native here. Alice goes native there. Okay, so far we're the same. She likewise tells them the "truth" about you like she sees it. How does she see it?"

Ronnie does the honors. "She thinks we're underachievers, that we indulge our desires too much and waste time on disgusting pleasures like the [*spitting-choking-word*] when we should be making the world a better place. Something like that. She's nuts."

"Okay. Picture her now on a world full of people who think just like she does. Now put an interstellar fleet and weapons of mass destruction in their hands."

Ronnie pales. "Oh my god. What do we do?"

Mizi pipes in, "Sex. We could have sex."

I look at her. "Sex in a crisis is such a cliché. Did you get that from the movies?"

"In part. But I also have found, as I get better at replicating the inner biology as well as the outer shape of humans, that I become both more alert and more relaxed myself during and after sex."

You know I'm deeply involved in interplanetary conquest, because that inner biology thing goes right by me. "Yea, okay, well, after sex, we gotta figure out how to enslave the Earth before the Earth enslaves us. Unless you have some secret weapon that you've been keeping from me, you green-eyed monsters, you."

So, after sex with a green-eyed monster—don't knock it till you've tried it—we got down to business. Enslaving, that always backfires, with uprisings and rebellions and everybody stashing their booty in Switzerland. Switzerland, that's the model we have to use. Small, but not particularly opinionated. Lots of spas for your rich and powerful, not to mention numbered bank accounts. We need to become a kind of interstellar Switzerland. If we've got your treasures stashed for you, you are not gonna blow us up.

Only thing is, Switzerland already exists for people to hide their illicit money. But weapons of mass destruction, nobody on Earth wants to keep them, but nobody wants to get rid of them either. We could offer a secure hideaway for anything too ugly for the treaty inspectors' aesthetics. You may shudder, but when I explain the proposition to Ronnie, she don't got a problem with it. Prob'ly, in part, because your deadly diseases that would wipe out the whole western hemisphere will not make a Blob so much as sneeze. Radioactivity can't make hair they don't have fall out, and if it could do some other damage, they don't seem too worried.

Ronnie does have some conditions. She don't want them building anything here. It's all got to be prefab, and then they just oversee placement and the locking up. But no building using stuff from the planet. Drop, lock, and leave.

Anyhow, I assign a single weapons-loving country to each of the top Blobs, so's each of them can swear she ain't discussed this with nobody else. Me, I call the President back. I am so impressed with myself when the President takes my call, no questions asked, but boy, does it make me lose respect for him.

"Mr. President, sir. I think the Blobs will agree to a little storage compound if you still want one."

"I knew I could count on you, Rose."

"I had to tell a couple of little white lies. I hope you don't mind."

"Now, now, Rose. I'll bet they weren't really lies. You simply told what we call in politics 'relative truths.'"

"Well, relative to the truth, I didn't say we wanted to store weapons of mass destruction. I said it was surplus food additives. See, they LOVED the candies and cakes you sent, especially the ones with bright artificial colors and imitation flavors. Imitation strawberry anything was a big hit. I said America was the world's supplier of fake flavors, and we wanted to stash some off-planet so, in case of an emergency, there'd be enough to keep the world in soft drinks and jelly donuts till the crisis had passed. They said it sounded like a very sensible plan and what could they do to help, so I told them to mark off someplace we could put the stuff and they wouldn't even know it was there. Was that right?"

When I worked for that phone-sex company, I always wondered what the guys faces looked like when they came. Privacy and all that, I never saw it, only heard the breathing and knew I'd done my good deed for the day at $39.95 plus tax, of which I got half. Who knew weapons negotiations would cause a guy to finish so fast, or I'd a tried it sooner.

I'm telling you, I succeeded in bringing off yours and my Mr. President in less than a minute, and not only heard the breathing this time but saw the sweaty flush go right up to his hairline. Let me tell you, it ain't a pretty sight.

He tried to cover, and of course I could only see him from the shoulders up. But you can't hide from a professional. "Oh, Rose. Rose. Oh. You did so well. Your patriotism makes me weak with humility. You are a true American. You just tell me where to put it, and I'll take care of the rest."

Yeah, yeah. I dated a lot of guys like that. No dice. "Now, sir, you understand that the Blobs still don't want a bunch of humans hanging out here. They say you have to build the units on earth and lock them up there. Then you bring them here and drop them in a designated, isolated area, put your locks and seals on the compound, and leave, secure in the knowledge it will be there whenever you need it."

The Pres, he don't like this arrangement. He wants his barbed wire, he wants his troops, and he wants his SCUD missile launchers in the bargain. My Uncle Ignaz, he wanted to have it all his way, too. Married a sixteen year-old from the old country, figured if he never taught her English, he could tell her how it's gonna be and she wouldn't know to argue. The day she explained he was gonna have to get a girl friend if he wanted any of that kinky stuff, he thought he was the smartest guy on Earth. When he saw the photographs taken through the motel window, he was prob'ly smiling a bit like the Pres is now. "But Rose, surely you realize we can't just leave our bombs there without some kind of protection."

"Protection from what? What do the Blobs want with that junk? They wouldn't know what to do with weapons. They never had a war or even a fistfight."

"I don't know about this."

"Look at it this way. Having the stuff here is like having it on neutral territory. Think of it like a tax-shelter numbered bank account in Switzerland. Nobody can prove it's yours, or that it's even there. You can't get any more neutral than that."

The Leader of the Cradle of Democracy wants his bomb storage, and in the end, he'll take it any way he can get it. "Just so we get a place to store them." He's pouting, but he'll get over it. Or not. Not my problem.

Ronnie and the other Blobs, they have similar conversations with the earth's numerous powers great and small. Send us your un-fired, your poisonous, and your destructive. Every single country jumps at the chance to load up their unwanted weaponry, send it on ships to Unpronounceable in secret, put their junk in secure vaults, and then leave us to guard it all. How stupid can humans be? You have to wonder if climbing out of the swamps onto dry land was really worth the trouble.

Chapter 5
Pre-Menstrual Sinkhole

So a bunch of us is watching *The Invasion of the Body Snatchers*, laughing, and eating hot buttered popcorn. I don't know how these Blobs do it, but once they have tasted a dish, they can reproduce the look, flavor, and texture so perfect even your mother wouldn't know her own cooking. I made sure we got food and beverage dropped off as gifts from every nation who put a stockpile here, so the last few months have been a nonstop party.

Makes me wish I had a sample of Ma's tortellini. You know that's all they're eating now up in Heaven, the gods having tossed out that nectar and ambrosia crap the minute she walked into the celestial kitchen. Don't think that she'd want a rest from cooking in the afterlife. For her to enjoy herself in Heaven, you know she'd have to be making her scratch pasta at least part of the time.

Descartes, he may have said the dubious but pithy "I think, therefore I am," but I believe you when you say you think about as much as I believe you when you say no woman has ever complained before so the orgasm problem must be me. Nevertheless, all your male philosophy professors who run the eastern half of the male cosmos, the western half being overrun by your macho but brainless gunslingers, they all think Descartes was deep. I'm not saying they're wrong. I'm too busy laughing at the moment. I prefer my Ma's motto,

"I cooked, so shut up if you want to eat." Which is exactly what we all did.

I'm showing this movie here as part of an official Cultural Relations Awareness Project. I had to come up with the long, bland, bureaucratic title so's they'd process the paperwork and send the stuff, but here we call it CRAP. And it really does have some higher purpose. Oh yes. I want to give the Blobs some insight into what humans really think about alien species, hoping to impress that they should never, ever exercise their shape-changing skills in front of any of the military types coming and going with bombs and such.

This is another reason Blob Alice was the perfect choice for Ambassador to Earth. She's so uptight, she can't hardly shift herself to move, let alone change her color, texture, and smell the way a normal Blob can.

Body Snatchers ends, and I go for a bathroom break before the next installment of our marathon. We've been at it for three days straight now without leaving the suite, having polished off *Alien* and the ten sequels, all the Japanese Godzilla movies, and the Star Wars series, and what with all the laughing, the Blobs are little more than pink puddles on the floor.

When I return, the gals have recovered a bit, I guess, because they are now writhing all over the room as pod-plants. All the pods split open at once and a dozen copies of me come out smiling that deadly bodysnatcher smile. Good thing I already peed myself empty, that's all I can say.

I decide we need a change of pace, so I fish out some disks of my favorite soap opera, *The Happy Few*, which is really all about the miserable many. I pop one in and settle back for some serious vicarious emotional involvement. I've missed several months of episodes, or about a week of soap opera life, and I am not expecting any surprises. NASA is not the only one who can do folding stuff with time so that it passes at different speeds in different places.

Sure enough, Rafe Wilcox, the devastatingly handsome n'er-do-well ladies man played by the creamy-dreamy Mark Main, is just saying goodnight to Davenport Locklear, the schizophrenic heiress, played by some blonde, after a dinner they had been planning as I was leaving Earth for Unpronounceable. Rafe is angling for a night of sex, but Davenport thinks she's still a virgin.

The Blobs are not getting the point. They still think we're watching comedy. I explain that Davenport has a split personality, that inside her prim exterior lurks a wickedly sexual vixen. Ronnie, to my eternal disgust, suddenly splits into Siamese-twin Davenports and the vixen half starts to have sex with the prissy half, who is fighting and screaming, "No, no!" Meanwhile a Rafe-lookalike Blob is wandering around naked and scratching his head. Apparently his penis has fallen off and he can't find it. He keeps trying to remember the last place he put it and is looking around the room. The Blobs, they're having a fine old time, but I'm steaming. I shut off the vid before the sacrilege can go any further.

"This is art, you cretins. Art! You will never have a civilization worth destroying because you don't appreciate the glory of the creative spirit."

The Blobs all suddenly freeze and stare at me. Then Gaudi farts. The rest dissolve into giggling gobs of formless pink protoplasm.

I suddenly understand why the Blobs, they never bother to make movies or write books. They don't got to. All they have to do if they want to know what it feels like to be beautiful like Miss America, or to sing like Michael Jackson, or to just be making sunlight into sugar for a hundred years like a tree is to turn into one. The real thing.

I start to feel sorry for myself, stuck in the same old body with the pumpkin-shaped Bellicosa hips and the pumpkin-seed Delancy boobs. I always forget that feeling sorry for myself is Stage One PMS, Stage Two being, of course, when I realize my misery is in fact the fault of some nearby dearly beloved, whom I proceed to blame in a high piercing tone of voice that has been known to curdle milk in the refrigerator. After six or seven hours of that, my vocal chords give out, but I feel better.

Unfortunately, that's tomorrow. Today, I just feel fat and ugly and unloved. I go into the bathroom and lock the door. There is nothing for me to do in the bathroom, having already taken care of business, except be with myself. Your swamis and such, they would see this as a golden opportunity to plumb the depths of my soul. I would rather flush myself down the toilet. Not a possibility, what with the Bellicosa hips and all. So I improvise.

I grab something off the counter—turns out to be a tube of face cream—toss it in the bowl, and flush. It goes away. I feel a bit better. I grab all my make-up that don't do no good anyhow and toss it in a pile that half fills the bowl. It disappears in a swirl and a whoosh. What the heck. I drop my toothbrush, toothpaste, floss, and night guard in. I'm on a roll. I toss the soap in. It floats. I wonder if the soap will go down or keep bobbing back to the top. I flush with an empirical flourish, and the soap goes scooting through like it had a purpose at last.

I'm starting to think it's impossible to clog the thing. I start grabbing towels and am contemplating the furniture in the next room. Notice I am not thinking about myself no more.

There's a knock at the door. "Rose." It's Mizi. "Rose, what's going on in there?"

"I'm just flushing stuff down the toilet."

"What stuff?"

"Everything." I open the door and march past Mizi and grab my clothes.

"Any particular reason?"

"I don't like my life, so I'm getting rid of it. Lucky for me, these toilets of yours will swallow anything that'll fit in the bowl. Think of it as an experiment."

"Need any help?"

"You touch my stuff, and you go down with the detritus, Gumball."

So Mizi backs up and rejoins the others. I tromp back and forth with armloads, while the Blobs, having turned away from the screen, are now watching me like I'm the Movie-of-the-Week. Screw 'em. I'm on a mission, and with each flush, I feel lighter and happier.

The drawers and shelves and closets empty pretty fast. I got nothing left and I'm feeling that that's more than I want. I spy the communications console, march over, and haul it off the desk, not bothering to disconnect the cords. I just yank and don't look back. It presents something of a problem, because the screen is wider than the bowl. I make like Conan and lift the shebang over my head and bring it smashing down on the tank. It crumples, and with the parts that break off I beat the rest into the basin and press the button. Swoosh! and it's gone.

The gals go nuts, cheering and clapping and stomping. I turn to the bunch of them. "Okay, which one of you wants to go next?"

Gaudi gathers her gooey self up as big and important as she can. "As the senior member of this assembly, I think it is my duty to go first."

At this, the gals all jiggle with guffaws and proceed to rush the bathroom in a writhing mass. I stop them with a squawk. "Hey, if you want me to pull the plug on your miserable lives, you gotta give me something for my trouble. You seen my sister Alice on the news, right? Make yourself to look like her if you want my cooperation."

Talk about a lifelong fantasy come true. Alice after Alice steps daintily into the bowl only to be sucked out of sight in a roar of water and air. Several scream very effectively as they squish and submerge. My favorite, though, is Mizi, who can't scream because she goes down head first, may she rest in peace.

But after the tenth flush the fun starts to pale, and by the time the last one has been washed out of my life, I'm not only depressed again, I'm completely alone.

I'm staring down the drain and remembering when I was three or four, I had a favorite toy necklace of pastel-colored plastic charms, all Jello pinks and yellows and greens, you know, disgusting girlie-girl colors, which Alice tossed into the toilet one day and dared me to fish out.

I threatened to tell on her, whereupon Alice explained that she would say that I, Rose, had been flushing all kinds of things all day and Ma should maybe check Aunt Mizi's jewelry box. I pointed out to Alice that Ma wouldn't find nothing missing because I didn't touch Aunt Mizi's jewelry.

Alice smiled and said the box was empty all right because she herself had taken the stuff and hidden it in case I wouldn't play fair. Not only would I be punished for sending such treasures as the mother-of-pearl scorpion pin and the tourmaline-chip silver cross to a watery grave, but I also would have all my other plastic jewels taken away and never be allowed to have so much as a ring from the bubble-gum machine ever again.

Well, I cried, being only four and not knowing that crying only makes people kick harder. Alice shook her head and said not to be scared, she'd hold the flusher tight so it wouldn't go off accidentally and drag me down inside the toilet. Then she put one hand on the lever and picked up the plunger with the other.

I shudder to think what would have happened if Uncle Alphonse hadn't needed to take a dump right then. He fished the necklace out first, though I was never able to wear it after that, what with Alice telling her friends that he had fished it out after and then just rinsed it off. Still, I did learn an important lesson that day.

I am on the verge of some deep psychological revelation about why I don't let myself care about things, or people for that matter, when I am saved by a knock on the bathroom door.

"Go away! You can flush yourselves from now on."

Again the knock. Some people don't have an ounce of consideration, dontcha know.

"Hey! I'm in the bathroom, and I'll stay here as long as I want. You can go outside in the bushes if you're in such a hurry."

Tap-tap-tap yet again, and I've had it. I yank open the door, and there's Elvis. The old, fat Elvis. Break my heart.

"Hey, babe." Mizi's got that velvet voice down perfect. "You know, you don't want to spend too much time in the bathroom. According to statistics, it's the most dangerous room in the home."

Elvis puts his arm around my shoulder, leads me over to the bed, and tucks me in. My sheets have reappeared, the video console is back in its spot, and I'm sure all drawers are full of stuff again. I sigh and let myself drift away to Elvis playing the guitar and singing "Love Me Tender."

As I nod off, I notice he's not really playing the guitar. He's just making gestures with his hands while the fully blended sound comes out of his mouth. I realize these Blobs aren't so smart after all, the guitar being something even Bob-the-beautiful-but-brain-dead could play, and I fall happily asleep.

Chapter 6

Follow Your Blister

"What do you mean, I have to start working? I'm a goddam Ambassador. All I gotta do is be myself, you said yourself just two...weeks?...hard to keep track here...no, two months ago. Being myself does not include spying."

"Research, Rose. Not spying. Research. We have some very important and fascinating studies we want you to undertake."

Rainer Lichtendorfman, who runs the UN, he's supposed to be a diplomat, and he don't like me. I ask you, what's the point of being a diplomat if you can only get along with the easy people?

Now he's smiling at me, which means he knows the job that he wants me to do while I'm here on Unpronounceable—I tried to come up with a name a person can say, but Hell is taken—is not only not "fascinating," it's gonna be so dull I'd have to kill myself to keep from being bored to death.

"We sent you a package with some questionnaires. Did you get it?"

"A big box full of three-ring binders?"

"That's the one."

"I flushed it down the toilet."

"You what?"

"I was having a bad day, and the box was there, and the three-ring binders had a lot of stuff in 'em that reminded me of a physics class I failed in junior college, and well, I sent them wherever sewage goes."

"Three-ring binders do not flush."

"They do here. Everything flushes. Anything you can jam in the john just scoots on through without a hiccup. No signs on the ladies room door not to flush tampons on this planet. I don't know how they do it, but Blob plumbing is amazing."

"That is exactly what we need to know about!"

"Their toilets?"

"Their science, their technology. It's all there in the toilet. Describe it to me."

Me and my big mouth. Now they know about the toilets. Pretty soon they'll be wondering how things here just fix themselves and clean themselves. Me, I don't bother wondering, I just leave my dirty dishes under the bed or in the bathtub. Next time I look, they're back in the kitchen, all nice and stacked in the cupboards.

"I can't describe how the toilets work. I flush and walk away. You don't think I watch the crap going down, do you? That's gross."

"I'll send you a new set of forms. All you have to do is ask the questions and write down the answers. In addition, we're sending some specimen boxes. Put any insects or plants you can find inside and ship them back with the filled-in questionnaires."

"Didn't all those scientists who was here before me get samples? Why do I gotta do it again?"

"Apparently, they became confused and brought back things that other people had taken there from Earth. We ended up with all the specimens we sent to the Unpronounceable for them to study brought back to Earth in the specimen cases. We didn't get one genuine alien sample as it turns out."

"What? You mean the white rats and fruit flies you sent, instead of infesting this planet, got bounced back at you labeled "Blob rodent" and "Blob bug?" Me, I'm thinking that is too sweet to be an accident. Gaudi must've come up with that idea. I laugh.

Rainer makes a sour face. "At first we were afraid the [Unpronounceable] used some kind of mind control to confuse our representatives, but as there is obviously no control whatsoever being exercised over your mind, we have revised our estimate to two other possibilities. One, that the [Unpronounceable] can perfectly duplicate matter down to the molecular level, something our scientists insist is impossible. Or two, the people we sent there screwed up royally.

"We decided to ask you to repeat the experiment. Actually, it was Ambassador Alice who suggested you. If you send us genuine [Unpronounceable] matter, then we'll know it was an honest mistake. If you don't or if everything that comes back originated on Earth in the first place, that means the [Unpronounceable] have something very big to hide, and we will know to take appropriate action. Do I make myself clear?"

"Wait, wait, whoa there. What's that last bit, 'appropriate action,' mean exactly?"

"Don't worry, Rose. We'll do our best to bring you out before it starts."

"Hey! Maybe you don't know this, but just about every major power on Earth has a little storage facility here which I don't think they would appreciate losing to your trigger-happy human-supremacist evil-alien paranoia."

"I know all about the 'little storage facilities,' as you so diplomatically put it. In fact, all it would take is a small action here to set off a large chain reaction there. We wouldn't have to send any new weapons or soldiers. You've saved us the trouble."

For the first time, I'm thinking this Rainer guy is not so stupid. "You thought this up by yourself?"

"To be honest, Alice, the alien one, told me about the facilities and suggested using them to control her otherwise wayward and undisciplined fellow aliens."

"Oh, god. Rainer, she's nuts. They picked the looniest, most anti-social specimen they could find just to get rid of her. That's Alice."

"We expected no less, having done exactly that with you."

"Hey, in case you forgot, I didn't get picked. All the guys you picked failed. I'm here because I played the Lottery and lost. It was fate, not fatheads, that put me here."

Rainer just smiles and shakes his head, and I realize the Lottery was a set-up. And if they didn't draw my name out of the hat, that means they actually chose me, Rose Delancy, to be the patsy, expecting me to do exactly what I've been doing. I get desperate and try appealing to his humanity.

"Don't forget the American Indians, Rainer. Think how history will curse you if you destroy the Blobs."

"We've already figured out how to blame it on you, Rose. You see, what with showing them all those horror movies and the pornography and importing enough nuclear ordinance to destroy the Earth, and adding to that your aggressive dissatisfaction with how others have treated you throughout your maladjusted childhood, you naturally corrupted those innocent creatures and turned them into allies for your twisted crusade against your own world. We had to protect ourselves."

"This is more Alice, isn't it?"

"I want to thank you for sending her, Rose. I assume you had a hand in the choice, because of her name."

"You are right about something at last."

"Oh, I've been right about many things. I must say, Rose, you have certainly performed beyond my expectations. I couldn't have dreamed it would turn out so well. Gosh, look at the time. I have to go. The shipment will be there shortly, and we'll be looking forward to the results. Goodbye." And the bastard hangs up on me.

Chapter 7
Anyplace I Hang My Hate...

I've been suckered. I admit it. But what Secretary General Lickandbarfman don't know is, I have practice at being royally screwed, having grown up with someone who over the years refined psychological warfare to an art form. I have learned that once Alice has you cornered, you can't win so don't bother trying. It gets in the way of trapping the bitch into losing as much if not more than you do.

The only hard part is the seeming surrender. It must be complete and humiliating. I call the President. I am humble.

"Mr. President. I'm sorry to bother you. You've been so great to me, and I never appreciated it until now."

"Well, Rose, what a pleasant surprise. What brought this change about, if I may ask?"

"I just received a call from the Secretary General..."

He interrupts with a sharp look and tone. "Lichtendorfman?"

"Yes, sir." The *sir* is a nice touch, don't you think? "He is maneuvering some sort of coup and apparently, by being so, well, difficult, I think I've played into his hands. Played America into his hands. And, oh, I'm so ashamed."

"And you want me to do something about it? Rose, I don't know if the US can openly..."

My turn to interrupt. "Oh, no, no. I don't expect you to act for me. Like I said, you've already done so much. I made my own mess, and I've got to live with it. It wouldn't be so bad except that, for the first time in my life, I feel like what I'm doing matters. I don't want to ruin my chance to be somebody at last. So, I wanted to tell you, I'm going to do everything he asks, and hope he'll let me stay. Even if what I have to do isn't, well, America first, you know? I felt I should at least let you know."

"Yes, well, politics asks us all to compromise our ideals. I don't know what to tell you, Rose. I would much rather have it be you up there than some Old World snob or a Third World agitator, or..."

"Mr. President. You don't have to pretend you approve of me. The Secretary General told me. I was picked because I'm such a loser. I don't have any authority, and I'm well, a bit of a joke."

The Pres actually looked slightly embarrassed, which shows you what a good actor he is. He wouldn't be embarrassed if you walked in while he was having sex with his dog. His dog would be more ashamed, and with good reason.

I continue. "It's okay. I am a bit of a joke. Even my family will tell you that." I smile a sheepish, self-deprecating smile.

"You know, Rose, years from now, I bet you'll look back on this as a growing experience. You sound like you're really ready to join society instead of fighting it. If this is the new Rose Delaney..."

"Delancy."

"...I may just have a place for you in my administration when you come home."

By the time I get home, I'm hoping he's been impeached and thrown in jail with the sexual predators. "Gee, Mr. President. I don't know what to say."

"I'll bet Lichtendorfman isn't asking you to do anything too terrible. After all, the whole world is watching. What does he want?"

"Oh. I don't know if I should say..."

"Scruples are good. Most of the time. But Rose, the UN is supposed to be completely transparent to world leaders. And

I am..." He winks and smiles. God, he's good. "...a world leader. Or was the last time I looked."

I laugh. I'm good, too, when I want to be. "That's what I heard. Okay, well, he wants me to gather specimen samples from here and put them in special boxes and ship them back to Earth."

"I thought the team of scientists did that ages ago."

"Apparently, they all brought back the exact same samples other people had brought here from Earth on the previous trip."

"What? We spent millions for that project. As far as I know, we're spending millions more to study the stuff. Only now you tell me the rocks and such they got are all from Earth. How could anyone make such a stupid mistake? And where is all my money going?"

Careful, now. "You'd almost think they went out in a field here on Earth, picked up some rocks, and only said they came from space."

The President gets very still, like his neurons suddenly short-circuited. He must be thinking.

I wrinkle my nose like Alice does and look confused. "Of course, then, the ships would've been sent out and back practically empty. Somebody would've noticed that. Unless there was something else on board..."

The President's reptile brain considers this unforgivable scam and realizes he would've done it if he'd thought of it. Obviously, he's not the only fraud out there in politics. What a surprise. And as it takes one to know exactly how to capitalize on fraud, he smiles wickedly but buries the tracks. "No, no, Rose. It must have been some perfectly reasonable mistake. No, I wouldn't worry any more about it if I were you."

"I'm sure you're right, Mr. President."

"And gathering samples could be very educational. I'm sure it will be good for you."

"Thanks, Mr. President. I feel better about the whole thing. Really I do."

"One thing, Rose. Do you think you could hold those specimens until we have a ship with an American crew to retrieve it?"

"I'll do my best, but I don't want to lose this job. If I get a direct order from the UN to ship them, I have to obey, sir."

"Just keep me posted. I'm sure we'll figure out something."

Now somebody who trusted other humans would think the President was gonna call the UN and righteously expose what he now thinks is a scam perpetrated on the peoples of the world. But the President, he's gonna call the UN alright, and he'll talk to Lickylickman, but only to congratulate him on how completely Rose Delancy, me, has been neutralized. Yes, every word of submission will be passed on, and then, as an aside, the President will also remark oh-so-casually about the rock business being mighty clever and wonder what exactly they did ship back and forth to Unpronounceable, hmm?

Licklockandload, he will know that he didn't concoct no scam, but he'll likewise know the President would never believe any denial. So he'll admit it. Later he'll start looking for the one who put that scam over on him, because that is after all the most logical explanation. No one really thinks a non-industrial, lotus-eating culture like the Blobs could transform matter as easy as passing gas, let alone keep such ability from the shipboard sensory apparatus poking their electronic noses around Blob-space.

So while his suspicions have been distracted from Blob-land, we must pull a fast one. For that I need a brain trust, but all I got is Mizi, Ronnie, and the gals. When I explain the whole mess, Gaudi is smug, because she had the Rose-gets-picked-cuz-she's-a-loser plan pegged. I ignore her, though I do cough up some phlegm coincidentally at that moment and, having no spittoon, decide she will do nicely. While she dodges the bullet by splitting in two, I point out that their own gal, Alice, is the one who came up with the plan that has us by the short hairs.

Gaudi collects herself and points out, "Seems to me you're the only one with hair, Rose, short or long. We, as you may have noticed, are perfectly hairless. Your problem, I'd say."

"Oh, really? Well just exactly whose idea was it to give the scientists Earth-identical samples?" Gaudi looks smug. "Don't you get what they'll do if they figure you can trans-whatever matter? You saw the movies. What do you think he meant by "appropriate action?""

Ronnie pipes in, "We can't send them any samples from here in their true state."

"I figured as much, Flubber. But when the new sample case arrives, something alien-like has to go inside. Any ideas?"

Naturally they have many ideas, all of them bad. Ronnie has the worst. "I think we should just tell the humans to go away and never come back."

"Idiot. What have I been saying to you about telling humans they can't have something, even if it's something they don't want? Even if it's something as worthless and miserable as this lump of rock you call home? Can't you gals at least tell me what the problem is with just tossing some dryer lint and a couple of roaches in the boxes? You have to have junk."

"Actually, no. We don't. Everything on the whole planet is interconnected."

"Spare me the mumbo-jumbo." I pick up a jelly bean pebble. "What would happen if you just let them take this?"

"They couldn't."

"Of course they could. Put it in a box on a ship, cross the fold, and voila, it's gone."

"Rose. It really is attached. Like a giant rubber band, only energy. They could jump through hyperspace with it. But when they came back out into C-space, the 'rubber band' would still be connected and bring the jelly bean back."

"It don't snap?" I could use one of these rubber bands for my hair.

All the Blobs, they shake their heads.

"It slingshots the whole ship back this way? How fast?"

Ronnie shrugs. "Your humans would be jelly."

Then Gaudi chimes in all happy with the prospect of catastrophe. "Unless the pebble punches through the ship and comes back alone."

Ronnie nods. "Either way, everybody on board dies."

"Then how come Alice can go to Earth, huh? Is she interconnected?"

"Only somewhat. Something happened to Alice. We don't know what, exactly. We think it had something to do with human contamination. There was that [*spitting-choking-word*] the businessman from Earth went to. It's a kind of communal bath, and well, the water was not properly sanitized afterward. Who knew human contamination would be so strong? Anyway, it was in the very next bath cycle that Alice was conceived."

"That can happen? Like my gramma warning me about getting pregnant by sitting on a dirty toilet seat?"

"Apparently, yes. So Alice is in part, well, human." I'm nodding, "So that explains her twisted nature." Which gives me an idea. "Okay, so you need something contaminated by humans. I'm human. Don't I contaminate anything?"

Ronnie rolls her eyes. "All the time."

"Like what? How?"

"Like you eat, and then you go to the bathroom. That stuff that comes out of you, not pure at all."

"My shit? Can you re-form it to look like rocks and plants without purifying it?"

"I suppose. But, ugh. Why would we want to?"

Mizi is smiling a Blob smile, which means her surface is shimmering. "We recycle Rose's shit, fancy it up and send it to Earth in the sample boxes."

Everybody's smiling now. Especially me. I'm picturing the great minds of Earth pawing through my doo-doo like my Aunt Lorena's Miniature Schnauzer used to do. He'd crap in the house when he was bored just so's he could play with it.

Gaudi, as usual, is the party-pooper. "This will not fool them for long. It's just another temporary fix."

I know she's right, and I hate it. "What we need to do is make Blobs the darlings of the Earth so that they stop asking questions. How to do that with grotesque lumps of pink protoplasm, I haven't a clue."

The planet itself is okay, but you'd have to like the Riviera to go for the place. Me, I hate the beach. But for most humans, the Mediterranean island sun-filled watery-wonderland kind of landscape here could inspire wonder. And condo-lust. If even one person was able to get himself a beachfront villa of his own, the Blobs would join the Dodo quicker than you could say "real-estate development."

This is why my policy is no permanent Earth-born residents. Ever. Except me. And people I like. So there'd be maybe three of us, if I can find somebody I can stand and they have a dog.

Mizi sighs. "I can't take all this thinking. I need a [*spitting-choking-word*]." She turns to me. "You want to come?"

"Do I look like I want to lose all my skin and go back to Earth in a hospital ship, writhing and screaming in pain the whole way?"

"That's one option, but it strikes me as a masochistic one."

"Hey, I don't think the last two guys picked that dish, either, but that's the bad sushi they swallowed."

"Who knew from what they told us they couldn't make more skin like a normal person."

"I can't make skin, and I'm normal."

"That's not what I hear."

I chuck a shoe at her. "What about all the screaming 'Stop! Stop!' What did you think they meant?"

"We thought it was in fun, like a child who wants you to tickle it, but tells you to stop the minute you start."

"Okay, okay. We've been over this, and I forgave you for flaying them. But why me, when you know my skin can't grow back?"

"You don't have to worry, Rose. We worked it out so it'll be okay for you."

Did you ever have a cousin like my cousin Lenore? She liked to cook, but somehow, there'd always be a revolting surprise in every batch of cookies she made. She'd make your favorite chocolate drop cookies because she heard you were coming over. You'd be eating her chocolate drops when suddenly you'd bite and a clove of garlic would have you gagging. My Great-gramma Ronnie would yell at you for spitting out your food instead of at Lenore, who always claimed these little pranks were accidents. How many accidents does it take before a pattern emerges? I should add she's on her fourth husband, two of them having passed away and the third having supposedly run out on her never to be heard from again. Think what you will, I eat no food in her house that I do not prepare myself.

Blob Ronnie pipes up, cutting off the happy reminiscences. "We won't let the [spitting-choking-word] remove all your skin, Rose, just the dead skin. You've got a lot of it, you know. It's even caked in the cracks of your wrinkles."

"Those are not wrinkles; those are creases."

"And you've got little bugs that live in there eating the dead skin."

"I do not."

"You do."

"I dare you to show me a single bug on my body."

"They're microscopic."

"Then how do you know they're there?"

"I can see them."

"You can see that small?"

"If I want to."

"Well, don't. It's perverted, looking at someone so close you can see her bugs. My wrinkles must look like the Grand Canyon."

"Creases."

"Whatever."

"Are you coming?"

I sigh. Being an ambassador is too much work. I could use a nice warm bath. "Can I bring my Barbie?"

Chapter 8

Even Jersey Girls Get the Bliss

Ronnie has some transubstantiating to do, so Me, Mizi, and Gaudi head for the [*spitting-choking-word*]. I don't understand why, if they are just baths, they don't call them "baths." I'm calling them baths. We head for the baths, Maurice's warning ringing in my ears like it was yesterday. With every step I'm getting more scared.

"You may have worked it out in theory, but it's literally my skin if you don't get it just right. You gals should maybe go without me."

Gaudi shrugs, though it's more of a rolling bulge, like when your tongue pokes into your cheek and feels around. "What's the difference if you die in a burning [*spitting-choking-word*] bath or a firestorm of nuclear fallout when the humans attack? Your life is miserable, and death couldn't come too soon." She had me there.

We go to the edge of town and enter this spectacularly arched corridor that winds upward on one side and downward on the other. I can't tell if it's built or natural. Their buildings are hard to tell from nature most of the time. Compared to these folks, Frank Lloyd Wright built houses that was pure Vegas

We go down a ways and then step inside this huge vaulted cave cathedral. In the center is a large wide pool. Light steam floats a few inches above the surface. But even with a ceiling above our heads and the smoky blanket on the surface, the water has a sparkle in it that is pure sunshine. There are other Blobs around the pool, but nobody goes in or even dangles a limb.

Just before we join the circle, Mizi pulls me aside and whispers. "You'll hear a sound like a gong. That's when we go in. The water at that point is safe. But Rose, here's the thing; you have to get out when you hear the second gong. The water will change after that, and your skin will not be able to take it. Get out and go up that ramp," She points out a steep ramp curving up the inside of the dome to the top, "and you can wait for me up there."

"How long?"

"It depends. Until the [*spitting-choking-word*] is over. You'll hear a third gong. Just remember, second gong…"

"I'm out of there, skin and all."

"Exactly."

We join the circle, where everybody's silent and still like in church, and I'm feeling a bit cranky. I hated church, sitting quiet and getting bored and not being able to talk or even scratch. But hey, I'm the emissary from Earth. So I suffer in silence for a while.

Then I hear a gong, and the Blobs all slide into the pool. They keep going until they are completely underwater. They float lazily around the water like perfect pink globules. I stand at the edge and just watch, mesmerized by the lava lamp impersonation.

I decide what the hell. The only way I'm getting up the nerve to go in is to do it quick. Diving may not be in keeping with the solemnity of the occasion, but I never let that stop me before. A lesser person might go so far as to do a cannonball right into the middle. Not this ambassador. I lift my arms over my head and make like a swan.

The water is nice and warm without being hot. It smells good too, like fresh herbs or the air after the rain. I tread water in the middle and watch the Blobs wobble and rock from the eddies. I realize nobody has come up for air since they went in. Blobs must be able to breathe underwater. I figure I'll join 'em for a minute. I hold my breath and dunk.

The Blobs are translucent. Pink and, well, don't say I said so, beautiful. They float around me and by me in a hallucinogenic slow-motion dance. After a couple of minutes, I notice I'm not out of breath. I figure I'm having some hypoxia fantasy, so I pop to the surface and take a breath. A normal breath. It's not like I'd held my breath at all.

I go under again. I stay there forever. I'm a mermaid. I'm a fish. The translucent, glowing forms hang all around me. I'm in a womb surrounded by giant eggs. I'm a baby salmon in a mountain stream. I'm among the planets in weightless rotation around the sun.

A gong sounds.

I'm Atlantis at the bottom of the sea surrounded by jewels nonpareil. A Blob is pushing at me. My skin tingles. Something I can't recall teases my brain. My eyes are on fire. I am with the lava at the core of the Earth. My insteps itch, my inner thighs too. I can't be bothered to scratch. I am there at creation the moment before the Big Bang. The Blob, one minute she's pushing me to the side and the next minute, POP, I'm inside. Her outer membrane just enveloped me.

My skin cools, everything cools, and I'm still, inert like dreams where you try to run but you can't. I'm not scared, just stopped. The water outside is fizzing now. Sizzling on the edges of the Blobs. Two Blobs become one. Then another joins. Soon the pool is one Blob. Me, too. I see it as if from the outside, but I'm at the heart of one giant glowing crystal mass. A crystal ball with a flaw. Me. This makes me sad.

Another gong. No more fizz. The water is still. It's all pulling apart, one from the other, separation, and I am floating alone. Alone, untouchable, unlovable. I swim to the edge and climb out. A beautiful experience, and I'm depressed as hell. God Rose, you are fundamentally fucked up.

The Blob who saved me turns out to be Mizi. Who else. She gets out and doesn't say a word to me. She just heads up the spiral ramp. Figures.

I follow. What else can I do? We go higher and higher until we reach the top, just under the vaulted dome ceiling. Arches open to the outside, and a ledge wide enough to stretch out on cantilevers out over the world. You can see out 360 degrees around. Around the edge are Blobs sitting alone or in small groups. They're not talking, though. They're just sitting looking out.

Mizi motions, and I go over. We sit and look over the landscape. I'd rather not look. I'm feeling so low, I do not want to be this high. I never had suicidal tendencies, but I prefer not to tempt my natural stupidity when it comes to survival. My eyes focus on the distance, the sea and the mountains.

Then I notice the pattern. It's not a pattern like Butterick or like polka dots. It's the land itself. It's telling me something, like it sees me and will keep me safe. So I relax and breathe. I didn't realize I was holding my breath. And get this. When I breathe, the landscape changes. Not changes as in "moves." Changes in meaning. Soon the landscape is saying, Life is Good. And then it's saying, I Love You. And then it's saying, Rejoice.

Rejoice.

I start to cry. I haven't cried since the fourth grade when Mrs. Harper cast me as the witch and then everybody laughed when I insisted I should play Gretel. I was a magnificent witch because I knew I was supposed to be Gretel. It was the only praise I remember getting from Aunt Mizi. "Rose, you were one helluva witch. Just shows that everybody's got a talent."

I'm still crying, and the landscape is smiling back, Rejoice. I don't want to be the witch, but I'd rather be the witch than nothing. And if that's my talent, Amen. I'm ready to face the music. I look away from the landscape, and sure enough, Mizi is still there.

Everybody else has gone. I must've been crying a long time. Mizi is twiddling four tentacles in a kind of dance. It's a happy dance, so I guess I didn't screw up so bad.

"I forgot to get out at the second gong, so I guess you really saved my skin."

Mizi starts dabbing me all over. I've seen Blobs doing this to each other before, but I couldn't tell if it was hostile or playful. I decide to give Mizi the benefit of the doubt after what she did for me, so I don't push her over the edge.

She keeps it up and starts talking, "It was a magnificent [*spitting-choking-word*]. We made two babies. Two. You were a wonderful presence."

"Babies? I took part in an orgy, and you didn't even tell me?"

"You were supposed to get out. It was just supposed to be a cleaning for you. Besides, it doesn't always produce babies. They are very rare. That is why two is marvelous. The Blob you call Carmella, she was there. She's a poet. She'll probably make a song about it."

"A song about what exactly?"

"I'll sing it to you if she does."

"Just so you translate it first. I might think you were choking on a fishbone and administer the Heimlich maneuver otherwise."

Mizi laughs. We turn and look out over the landscape for a while. The landscape doesn't make a pattern anymore.

"This is a wonderful place."

Mizi turns to me. "Did it speak to you?"

"Yes."

"What did it say."

"Life is good. I love you. Rejoice." I laughed, and Mizi wiggled with such pleasure she looked like a giant pink puppy.

"I knew it. Well, and how does it feel, your skin?"

I touch my cheek. My face is so soft. "I never had skin this soft. Even when I was a baby." Every touch was so pure and alive, my fingertips were affected, too.

As we walk back to my place, I feel the air, the ground, the light like never before. When I get home, I ask for a mirror. I kept breaking all the mirrors the first week, and so they finally stopped coming back. Now I want to see if I could actually notice the effect of the bath.

Sure enough, it is as if five years has dropped away. Then I notice my body, which has trimmed down to a svelte curviness with no cellulite. I look harder. Not one lump of cottage cheese. Smooth as can be. And my boobs, they never were much, but they have a fullness, a perkiness they haven't had since I was fourteen.

I run and grab some of my clothes and put them on. Two sizes too big. I don't understand. I say so to Mizi. "I don't understand. I eat twice as much junk as I did on Earth. I should look like a Blob."

Mizi shrugs, "The calories and nutrients adjust so you only get what you need, no matter how much you eat."

The calories...adjust...?

"Rich and famous people on Earth pay fortunes to go to beauty spas and fat farms that don't work, paying though the nose so's they can pretend to themselves they look better. If anyone ever figured out how to do both in one and deliver results like this, that person would rule the rich, which is the same as ruling the world, only without needing an army..."

Of course, you figured it out hours ago. Me, I get the idea right here.

Chapter 9
Hooray for Hollywood

I never had a big idea before. Not that ideas is hard. You just think them. It don't take no longer to have a big idea than a small idea, like maybe I can fix my broken fingernail with Superglue, or even a bad idea, like when I tried buttering the bread before I put it in the toaster. But a really good, really big idea, that takes perspective, which don't usually happen to someone with my IQ and life experience. Only, being an interplanetary ambassador, that don't happen to a person like me neither, and being an ambassador to Unpronounceable certainly has been an experience.

So here I am, trying to save this Blob planet by turning it into the galaxy's greatest spa. Except Blobs is not exactly an appealing name for a spiritually enlightened people, and Fart-Sound World is not the name a market research firm would suggest if you was starting up a fat farm to cater to your rich and famished. We could change the name, but to what? "Spa World" sounds like a theme park with rides. Fountain of Youth implies you could just bottle it and send some home. We need the ultra-rich and ultra-powerful to think loung-ing on our deck chairs is even more *ne-plus-ultra* than cashing chips in Monaco or skiing the Alps.

We got another problem besides the name. Everybody on Earth knows all the gory details of every single cultural exchange fiasco leading up to the Lottery that picked me as an ambassador in the first place. Unpronounceable has got a reputation, which I have encouraged in order to keep humanity from showing up for a visit and moving in.

So not only do we gotta change the name, we gotta change the image. This has to become the only place that is Someplace if you are Somebody, and too expensive if you are Nobody, like a government bureaucrat.

I'm the first to admit the job's too big for me. We need the expertise of people whose sole purpose in life is to sell tasteless trash to your unsuspecting public and make them happy to pay for it. We need Hollywood. The thing is, to get from Hollywood, you gotta give to Hollywood.

I call the four major studios and leave a message saying the Blobs is interested in seeing a movie made and does any of them want to be the first and only studio to shoot a space flick actually on another world. Using alien actors. Real aliens. I tell them to call my assistant, a gal named Mizi.

I figure I better tell Mizi about her new job. She's about as happy to hear the news as I was to find out you don't just get your period once, but every single goddam month for the rest of your life. Unless you get pregnant. Oh goody.

I do what I can to convince her. "Hey. Hey! These are Hollywood people. The folks who make the movies we've been watching. Think what an opportunity for amusement I'm offering you. They'll try to do deals with you. They'll flatter you till you'll turn into Blob mousse from all the laughing."

"I'm not flattering anybody."

"You, you can say anything you want back to them, and they'll treat it like the wisdom of the ages. Because if they hang up, some other studio gets the deal."

"Anything?"

"Just remember, we get script approval and final cut."

"Why?"

"My former boyfriend, Bob, was a sometimes working movie actor, and talking about himself and his business was all he did when he wasn't at the gym. Script approval means we can make sure the Blobs come across all cuddly and lovable."

"Yuck."

"And we want final cut because they won't respect us if we trust them."

"Well, that, at least, makes sense. Okay. I'll do it."

"But remember, you're my assistant."

"What do you do that I am assisting? Seems to me you sit around all day, and when you're not eating you're shouting or screwing."

"Exactly. I can't do any work if I'm important. Only assistants actually work. There has to be a whole string of useless people here who make boneheaded decisions or they will not take us seriously. Once you do the deal, I'll okay it and Ronnie will sign off, and soon there'll be a hundred fruitcakes from California swarming over the city."

"Can't we just explode the nuclear weapons in the storage facilities now and get it over with?"

"Not yet. After I get my revenge, you can blow yourself to bits."

"Uh, about those storage facilities..."

"Not now. Right now, I've got noses to rub in doo-doo, and a little suffering on your part is necessary, so get over it." Mizi shrugs, and I take that for a yes.

Next I hunt up Ronnie.. "Ronnie, we need to design a luxury spa with two-room suites for the guests and some smaller cubicles for assistants. And it has to be something humans can find their way around, not something that looks like globs of frosting that a demented child used to build a sand castle."

"No problem. I'll use the layout on the Parcheesi board one of your predecessors left behind as the floor plan. How many you figure will come?"

"We set the limit to twenty. More humans would just ruin the place. Plus twenty is exclusive. No wannabes. Just the cream."

"I'll get to work on it."

"The first people will be the movie people. Keeping it to twenty including actors will be harder to enforce, but I intend to be the great bitch from hell about it."

"And how will that be different from your normal bitch from hell?"

I ignore the small talk. "The big problem is the spa staff. We can't have human staff, or they would have to be here permanently."

"One permanent human is already too many."

"So Blobs have to be the servants. Only you take too much getting used to looking the way you do."

"We could look like humans, the way Mizi does for your sex games."

"No, no. Mizi is too good at it. And too sexy. It will scare them. Remember *Body Snatchers*? No, you have to shape change only a little, and don't color change at all. Here." I pull out my Barbie and Ken dolls. I really do play with them in the bath. "This is what you all should look like, leastways every Blob who works in the spa. You as Grand-Poohbah-Blob can retain your disgusting shapelessness. But the rest must make like the dolls and never wobble."

"Ken has no penis. And Barbie has no nipples."

"And neither will your people. Just like plastic dolls in every detail."

"Nobody's going to want to do this."

"Think of the humor factor. You will see some pretty amazingly stupid behavior. Enough to keep you laughing for millennia. And it will effectively make Bliss hands-off for any would-be imperialist."

"Bliss?"

"Yeah. Blob-land, or that unpronounceable farting noise you guys use as a name won't do for a high-class spa. Bliss, we will have the Hollywood PR people explain, is what that fart-noise means in human language."

"You are depraved."

"I know."

Just then, Mizi rolls in, all stiff like a scoop of pink sorbet. "Hollywood people. Do you humans let them reproduce?"

"Humans would even let you reproduce, Mizi. A government can commit almost any crime against humanity as long

71

as they let even the most vicious and feeble-minded 'good citizens' have as many babies as they can find partners to provide."

My phone beeps. I scoot Ronnie and Mizi against the wall so they can listen and not be seen. It's Lichtendorfman.

"Rose. What are you up to? I'm getting requests from Hollywood film studios for permission to go to Unpronounceable."

See, I even got him calling it Unpronounceable. I shake my head. "Bliss."

"Huh?"

"Bliss. I finally got around to asking one of the Blobs..."

"I wish you wouldn't call them that."

"...what the fart-noise they make actually means if it was translated into English. I'm such a dope I never thought to ask it." This is a lie. I did ask. They told me it means, "The place where we live and you don't." I continue, "Can you believe I was so dumb?"

He can't resist the bait, even though going for it will make him lose his train of thought. "Actually, Rose, that comes as no surprise."

"Yeah, well, like my Great-Gramma Ronnie used to say, 'Even a blind sow finds an acorn now and then.' What can I do for you, Mr. Secretary-General?"

"These calls all claim that they have been invited to Unpron...Bliss to discuss making a movie there."

"That was Ronnie's idea. She saw all those alien horror movies and got all starry-eyed. Then she watched the Oscars award ceremony and announced that that was her destiny. She insisted I make the calls. I figured there'd be no harm in asking. They're supposed to submit their scripts by the end of the week."

The Blobs are puddles and oozing under my shoes. I ignore them and concentrate on the oversize pores on Lichtendorfman's nose to keep me from laughing along.

"I don't think this is a very good idea."

"You and me both, sir. You can tell the Blobs no dice on the movie, and it would suit me just fine."

"You are the Ambassador, Rose. You can tell them."

"Okay, Mr. Secretary-General." I smile, don't put up even a little fight. That surprises him. "I'll tell Ronnie no dice. Movies is for humans. And you can tell the Hollywood people you won't let them accept the invite. Is that all?"

He looks concerned. He can't believe I'm giving in so easy. He don't understand, I don't have to fight this one. Warner Brothers or Sony or Fox will fight it for me. All I gotta do is pick.

Chapter 10

The Royal Treatment

Sure enough, nobody in Hollywood worries about a little problem like the UN saying "no" to them. They sic their PR machine on poor Liplesswonder, announcing to the world they have been invited to make a movie on the alien world with real aliens in it, and get people so excited to see it, all the UN can do is roll over and act like they enjoy it. Meanwhile, the studios all bust their chops to churn out the most exciting, most original, most action-packed space opera they can concoct with the considerable resources at their disposal.

Nobody in Hollywood actually sends a script. They send something called a "treatment." A treatment is a description of the story, maybe fifteen pages instead of a hundred. We get one from each of the Big Four. I lay in bed and start in on the pile. Two pages, and I realize I am being selfish. I call together fifty of my closest friends, and to get in the spirit, we make it a beach party, Mizi being such a fan of Elvis.

Soon we are lounging on blankets under a coral pink sky. No sand. The beach looks like pretty colored pebbles and shells that are actually jelly beans and assorted candies so's we have something to sustain us as we tan. And when I say "we" I mean yours truly, Blobs naturally being a sunburn pink that would mean skin cancer in you and me.

I assign roles. Everyone participates. If they don't play one of the characters, they become the scenery. I read aloud.

The first treatment is about a handsome spaceship captain who is marooned on a planet and taken in by kindly aliens. Earth didn't know there was life on this planet, and the company he works for is a space mining operation. They are planning to crack the whole planet open to suck out the valuable ore at the core. Even after our hero reports that it's inhabited, the evil mining magnate doesn't care that there are people on the planet. The noble captain has to fight off the invasion and save the poor sweet Blobs from annihilation. He succeeds, but dies trying. The Blobs make him a hero and erect statues to him all over the planet.

The next one is about a handsome spaceship captain who has become jaded and bitter. He lands on an alien planet looking for valuable gems to trade. He is in debt to an evil underworld warlord and has to score big on this trip or he's a dead man. Sure enough, he finds a mother lode, but before he can return with his riches, he gets deathly ill with a dreadful brain virus that destroys the mind completely. The friendly native people nurse him back to health so well that instead of becoming a vegetable, he's whole and even healthier than before. His scars, both outer and inner, are healed. They refuse payment, even though their lives are poor and hard. He realizes if he returns with his riches, the planet will soon be swarming with miners and the Blob-people with their delicate ecosystem will be destroyed. He decides to return empty-handed, with stories about how worthless the planet is, even though it means his death.

The third treatment is about a handsome spaceship captain, a grizzled veteran who has fallen on hard times. He is hired by a young, beautiful heiress to take her to a mysterious planet for reasons she will not reveal. They fight about everything, but are obviously attracted to each other—he to her sleek classy looks and she to his savvy at eluding space pirates and government inspectors alike. When they arrive at the planet, they are met by swarms of friendly little Blobs, who are awaiting the heiress and her supply of oregano. Apparently oregano is a highly potent hallucinogen for these harmless innocent creatures. The jaded captain is outraged. It turns out the heiress is a addicted to drugs herself, and has been blackmailed to be the courier for the drug kingpins. He helps her kick the drugs and then together they kick some butt, deposing the drug czar and defeating his armada single-handedly before falling into each other's arms.

The final treatment is about a handsome spaceship captain who works for an illegal drug ring disguised as a mining operation. Ostensibly prospecting on a newly discovered planet, our hero is really trying to find and smuggle away some native plants, which give humans a spectacular high and which is a thousand times more addictive than heroin. The captain's ship is in hock, and the only way he can keep it is to serve the evil drug lords, even though he despises himself for selling out. He finds the plants with the unwitting help of a gorgeous, buxom xenobiologist, who along the way shows him how the drug traffic is destroying the native people's peaceful, innocent culture. The captain takes on the drug dealers and the corrupt government officials to stop the drug trade and restore the native culture, winning the heart of the xenobiologist along the way.

By the time we are done, I have laughed so much I am jelly, and apart from the skin color and the hair, you can't tell me from the natives. The Blobs, they got out of hand by the end. Buxom, the script said, meaning big for a human female. Well, while humans top out at double-D cups, the Blob playing the xenobiologist would've needed double-J cups. What amazed me was how they stayed up there. Even Blobs have to submit to gravity. I guess they still have a few tricks I don't know about.

"Okay, ladies. Let's have some decorum. We need to give notes on these, tell them what we want fixed…"

"The ideas!" some wag calls out. This gets them all started.

"The writing!"

"The plot!"

"The story!"

"Hey, hey. Hey!" I silence them. "We need specific suggestions…"

"But, Rose. There's no fixing these stories. They're bad from start to finish."

"Not fix them to make them good, you pea-brained pink pudding head," I soothe. "I use the word "fix" as a metaphor."

"You wouldn't know a metaphor if it slapped you with a fine, put you in a pipe, and smoked you at the line of scrimmage singing, 'Rose is a rose is a rose.'"

"We have to make some very stupid but very self-serving suggestions, or they will think they can walk all over us when they get here. For instance, I think we should suggest that instead of a buxom xenobiologist, the heroine of number four should be a sexy but flat-chested ambassador."

This causes laughter that lasts more than five minutes. "Any other ideas?"

"I know. What if when the aliens take the drugs, they get a hard shell and can't wobble any more? Alice will hate it when she sees it."

"Now that's thinking with your lower nature. More, we need more."

"Can't we have a woman as the hero?"

"In a movie? Who would make this film? Even the Hollywood execs who are women are just one of the boys. And boys watch space movies so's they can bring their own private spaceship to ignition and blast off. They are not interested in a woman having a space ship of her own. Why would she ever need a man?"

This philosophical discussion has cooled the giddy atmosphere and allowed some Blobs to collect themselves. We get to work rewriting the treatments. At one point, Gaudi, as usual, objects. "Why do all the screen aliens have to be so stupid?"

"Why should we pretend you're smart when you're not? It's just a movie."

"Why should we pretend you're sexy and beautiful?"

"That's different. We want to arouse the males so they will have happy associations with Blobs. If you put me as I am in the flick, they will want to bomb the place."

"Well, we may not have much sense, but we do have taste. Can't we be less insipid?"

"Your taste is a matter of debate, but humanity's taste is not. This movie is for them. The sweetness has to be cloying, the morals have to be absolute, and the women have to be empty vessels waiting to be filled by the men, or people will not believe it's true."

A general retching sound assures me they have understood. We finish the rewrites and head back to the ranch where I beam them earthside. I go to rest up after all the laughing. I feel like I ran a marathon. My muscles ache, and my brain feels like mush. I grab a box of chocolates and climb into bed. I munch away contentedly knowing that I could eat the whole box and not gain an ounce of flab or produce a single zit on my chin. I'm actually thinking I could learn to like it here. Just goes to show what happens when you let your guard down.

Chapter 11

Parcheesi Interlude

Mizi has been watching too much Disney, and right now I'm playing Parcheesi with one of the hippos from *Fantasia,* which is almost like being with her in her natural state except for the tutu. And the ballet slippers.

Since I am a good friend, I am wearing a red cape like the nasty alligators, figuring I can dress the part even if I can't actually change shape.

Mizi rolls the dice but has no move. My turn. Only suddenly, one die shifts and has 5 dots instead of 4.

"Hey, no fair! You can't change the numbers on the dice just so's you won't lose."

"The whole point of playing a game is to play the game. If I lose, the game is over."

"No, the whole point of playing the game is to win by the rules to show how much better you are than all the losers. If you keep changing the rules to keep from losing, nobody ever wins."

"Exactly! Rose, I learned this from you! It's what we all love about you."

I pick up the board and hit the hippo over the head with it. "Love? Take that back!" I hit Hyacinth repeatedly with the Parcheesi board. "Take it back, you tub of mud-wallowing lard. Take. It. Back."

Mizi opens wide, snaps the board out of my hands, and swallows it. "You play by your rules. I play by mine." The hippo smiles and waggles its eyebrows.

Now, this was not your ordinary eyebrow waggle. Nor was it an invitation to swamp-love eyebrow waggle. No. This was an I've-got-a-secret-and-want-you-to-drag-it-out-of-me eyebrow waggle. Don't ask me how I knew this. You hang out enough with somebody, you learn to read their eyebrows, I guess, even if they're a shapeless Blob most of the time.

"No, I am not playing Twenty Questions with you."

"You're the one who broke the Parcheesi."

What can I do but sigh? "Is it bigger than a bread box?"

A nod. "Times 20."

"Awww, the WMD storage. What did you bozos do?"

She bats those hippo eyelashes at me and tries to look all innocent. "We didn't like how unsettled the atoms in there were, so we helped them calm down."

"You 'calmed down' Earth's entire supply of nuclear material, is that what you're telling me?"

"Pretty much."

"And what do you think will happen when they come to collect some of it?"

Absentmindedly rearranging her tutu, she says, "You know how the agreements all said they were storing stupid stuff? Food additives and toilet paper?"

"I know, but what they sent was…."

She shakes her head.

I see it all now. "If and when they look inside, they will find exactly what the invoices say?"

A nod.

Now I'm laughing. You're laughing too, admit it. I love these Blobs. Just don't quote me.

Chapter 12
Flight or Flight

All too soon, Hollywood arrives on Bliss. There's way more than twenty cuz apparently assistants, hangers-on, and wannabes don't count as people, but as accessories. Not that the Blobs can't handle it, but I'm not so sure about yours truly. Now, I do not like humans, myself included, and have been blissfully happy, pardon the pun, seeing a total of zero ever since I landed. I'm thinking this time I won't mind them so much, seeing as how I've got the upper hand, but I forgot, being away from Earth so long, that there is no upper hand when dealing with humanity.

I hang back to appear aloof and all-powerful and let the Blob Barbies and Kens in white hospital gear do the meet-and-greet. Even seen at a distance, your first person off the shuttle rocket defines delusional self-importance, and everyone who follows manages to raise the bar until I'm sure the next one could only be a gibbering idiot.

I feel a tap on my shoulder. I turn and recognize that general, Griswald was his name, who got sent back in disgrace three or four ambassadors back. He's wearing a baby blue jogging suit, dark glasses, and fake wavy black hair, but it's obviously him. He alternates between smiling and posing like a Hollywood star, and twitching and skulking like a spy.

"Hello, Beautiful. I'm Gerald Gris...uh, Grant, Gerald Grant, actor." He winks at me. "I'm playing the President."

"Nobody wearing a cheap rug gets to call me anything but Madam Ambassador, Gerry. You got that?"

"Yes sir. I mean, Madam. Ambassador."

"I thought Charlton Gibson was playing the President."

"Change of plans. Last minute. I was called in to save the day."

"I didn't know any of the days was in trouble."

"Hee-hee. You'll see."

Then he winks at me again and saunters off. When he nears the hotel, suddenly he turns and makes like Rambo with his back to the wall before peering around the corner to see if the coast is clear.

I can't figure why he's back here, having been sent home screaming in a strait-jacket, or why he's using another name, like that would fool anybody. Not that I need to know why to torture him. I holler, "Griswald! Look out!"

He turns, dives for a buffet table laid out in the plaza, grabs a piece of fruit, pulls the stem out with his teeth and tosses it back where he was standing to splat on the wall while he ducks under the tablecloth. Every single Blob stops to applaud, and poor Griswald, he can't resist. He pokes his head out and sees all the cheering is for him. So he gets up and bows a few times, then picks his toupé out of the potato salad, plops it back on his head, and saunters off all nonchalant, dripping mayo and chunks of egg in his wake.

I turn away with a happy sigh to scan the assembled Hollywood types. They are all stylish and beautiful, except for the guy at the center of the largest group of yes-men and nubile women who is a paunchy, balding man in maroon velour sweats. He is the Producer, Dick Glick, and Mizi, now looking like a living Ken doll, is bringing him over.

"Dick Glick, this is Ambassador Rose Delancy."

"You're the Ambassador?"

"Yeah. You got a problem with that?"

"No, it's just nobody told me you were such a babe."

"Dick, can I call you Dick? I should tell you, flattery makes me violent. So knock it off."

"Say no more. I hate flattery myself. I am known throughout Hollywood for my down-to-earth sincerity. Isn't that right?"

I'd answer that question with a big wet raspberry, but he don't ask me. He asks the general throng around him, and they all make like those bobblehead dolls of Jesus, Mary, and the Magi my Aunt Laverne keeps in her car. I change the subject so's I don't barf.

"I see you met Mizi, my assistant. She…" And there I almost blow it. Glick eyes Mizi's Ken doll physique, and I have to backpedal. "…I mean, HE will take you to your suite. Later we'll go over the schedule, after you get settled."

Mizi gives me a look that's pure poison, and I smile arsenic right back. That's what I like about arsenic. You build a tolerance, and then it can't hurt you while everybody else is dropping like flies. Mizi, he/she sighs and turns to Dick and his fluffers.

"If you'll follow me, Mr. Glick."

Glick and company head off with Mizi/Ken for their private suites admiring, "Say, this place is swell."

I'm feeling pretty smug, dontcha know, which goes to show how anybody can get soft in the head. I turn and take a shot right between the eyes.

"Hello Rose."

He don't got no goop all over him, and his hair looks like it recovered. Otherwise, Bob standing there smiling at yours truly hits me like a PTSD/LSD/Past-Life-in-an-Inquisition-torture-chamber flashback. He should not be smiling after all the things I said to him. I was counting on that to keep him way away, as in the farthest corner of the Earth away from me, not right here on Bliss within swooning distance. I cannot think within 30 feet of his pheromone-packed physique, and I need my wits to pull off this scam.

"You. What are you doing here?"

He does that innocent shrug he used to practice for hours in front of the bathroom mirror. "I got cast. I didn't even have to audition. I'm playing the intrepid starship captain, Johnny Roman."

"Intrepid. That's a big word for you, isn't it?"

"Yeah, but it's got to be a good thing, since I'm the hero. You're looking good. I see you got that boob job after all."

I do not understand the comment, but then I probably don't have enough cells in my brain that is working now to understand much of anything. "Huh?"

"It looks great."

He smiles and steps closer so's I can get a better whiff of eau de Bob and lose a few million more brain cells. "Rose, you look swell."

Alarm bells go off, but I hit the "snooze" button. This is so not like Bob, or any other man I've spent more than five minutes having sex with, all warm and approving when they got nothing to gain. I lean into him, and we almost touch, which would lead ten seconds after to naked on the sidewalk, but the next shuttle has arrived, littering the planet with another Hollywood entourage, this one surrounding a woman dolled up in sequins and fur. But nothing can doll up that voice.

"Bob, sweetie. Can you give me a hand?"

Alice.

Bob starts to turn to her, and I yank him back. "What is she doing here?"

"Who, Alice? She's playing you." He uncurls my death grip from his arm before turning away. "Coming, sugar lips."

"Sugar lips?" When you find your ex-boyfriend is not only dating your sister but calls her "sugar lips" when the only nickname he ever came up with for you contains several four-letter words you would not find in your regular dictionary, that should be enough to absolve you of any and all crimes committed henceforward from now to the heat death of the universe.

Alice takes Bob's hand, glances my way to make sure I'm watching, which who can stop from watching a train wreck be it somebody else's train much less your own, and she pulls the Boob into a passionate kiss. I swear I can hear the steam whistling out of my ears. If I don't do something quick, my head will explode.

I bust into the producer's suite to find him already in his hot tub with thankfully enough bubbles to maintain the necessary decorum of Ambassador-to-Dick negotiations.

"She's my sister. She's not an actress."

"You let me be the judge of that, Rose. I tell you, the gal's a natural."

"Does she have to play me? Can't she play the twisted forces of darkness?"

"Don't you worry your pretty little head about that. When this is over, everyone on Earth will love you."

"I do not have a pretty little head, and I do not want anyone on Earth to love me. Not you, not the loving mother with three kids and a puppy, not the geezer who paints over the graffiti on his fence, not the climber breathing pure mountain air or gasping his last pathetic breath from an oxygen tank after falling over a cliff. I get to say what goes in this movie, and I want her out."

"Rose, you get script approval, location approval, and even final cut approval, but casting approval, that would belong to the UN guy."

"Lichtendorfman?"

"Yeah. Wouldn't give up the permit without the say-so on casting."

"And you just rolled over?"

"Well, yeah."

I would argue some more, but I gotta pack. And then go. So I head back to my place and start filling my old suitcase with my old clothes, not that they fit anymore, but a few months on Earth, and I'll gain it all back. Mizi comes in and talks into the little headset I got them all wearing.

"I found her."

I pause in my packing to grab the walkie talkie and flush it down the toilet. I'm almost done anyway, since I can't take any souvenirs from this hell hole without blowing up the ship. Souvenirs. How could I have missed that? I hit myself in the head.

"Listen, before I go, you should know I just figured out another big hole, the first one being that Alice could come here and ruin yet another planet, in this idea for spa world thing, cuz dontcha know everybody's gonna steal soaps and towels when they leave, which if they did would kill them and everybody else on board. But you can't get humans to stay in a place and not take something back, so maybe you need to have some cheap stuff made on Earth and then shipped here and then put locks on it, you know, like you're scared they'll steal it, which they will, so you can control what they take."

"Rose, you can't leave. Where would you go? Back to Earth?"

"Alice is here. I am leaving. It's not complicated."

"But once you're on Earth, and she returns, won't you be stuck with her forever instead of just two months?"

"Good point. I'm gonna hijack a ship and head out. Away. Don't ask me where I'm going. This way she can't trick you into telling and come after me."

"Your biology books call this a fight or flight response."

"I failed biology. Pass me my sex toys."

"I only mention it because I think you're looking at the wrong half."

"Huh?"

"You picked flight. Not fight. This isn't like you."

"Look, Mizi. I'll take on the whole world, but not Alice. The truth is, my Great-gramma Ronnie was right. I'll never beat her. I might as well admit it and save myself all the public humiliation."

"Rose, what about us?"

"You'll see. You'll prefer her to me just like everybody else."

"But she's so...fake."

"You're one to talk, mister life-size plastic Ken doll."

"Why don't we just have sex?"

"I'm not having sex with a sexless plastic toy."

"Since when did that change?" Mizi/Ken underscores his point by picking up one of the vibrators, turning it on and waggling it at me as it buzzes.

You know those rebus puzzles teachers torture kids with in elementary school. You see a couple of pictures and together they are supposed to add up to some other thing. I was never no good at them, but maybe school wasn't offering the right motivation, cuz right now I see two different things—plastic vibrator and plastic Blob—and they do add up big time. Not to a word, but an idea.

"Can you do that?"

Mizi smiles and turns the toy off, but the buzzing sound don't stop. Now it's coming from his pants. So I guess I'll stay here a little longer.

Chapter 13
Trailer Trash

So after a week of human infestation, which I have spent mostly in bed with a pillow over my head, I am finally on the movie set version of Unpronounceable, which is what I still call it in my head, Bliss being an imaginary place where everybody is happy and boring. We got every paradise cliché working here, so I'm wearing dark glasses to keep from going into a diabetic coma of the eyes. Lotsa giant pastel flowers, tall frondy greenery and grass, every blade exactly the same length and thick and soft as a goose-down mattress. For the buildings we used pictures from the Taj Mahal, Disneyland, and Ancient Greece all smooshed together in a new architecture style we call "Swami," which we are not telling anyone stands for "Shit Wobbly Aliens Make Irresistible." In the distance you got your snow-capped mountains littered with sparkling waterfalls on one side, and wide sandy beaches—no candy for these yahoos—on the other.

The minute I walk on to the set, several people hurry over from every direction, so I got no way to escape. One brings a chair and tucks it behind me like maybe I'm so exhausted from the two-minute walk over here that I'll fall faint on the floor from the exertion. I grab the armrests so she can't yank it away at the last minute and make everybody else's day, and climb up. It's one of those tall canvas director chairs that put your head just a tad higher than most everybody else like a king. I got a good view of the chaos, better than if I was standing, so I settle in.

As soon as I'm perched, another flunky puts a cold drink in my hand and asks if I want anything. "I want everything," I say, because saying what I want just guarantees that that one thing will never come my way, but by saying I want everything means that I don't actually get my hopes dashed from wishing and failing to get what I really want, and since "everything" includes lotsa terrible crap, I get nothing good or bad and they leave me in peace, which is a plus you should not knock until you've tried it.

But go figure, this flunky standing next to me just says, "Everything. You got it." And hurries off to get it. I can not imagine how she thinks she can do that, but I suppose everything is possible in Hollywood.

A lady in a suit holding a clipboard steps into my line of sight. "Hello, Rose. I'm Ellen Wishford of Wish For It PR." She's smooth in a not-one-hair-outta-place-perfect-makeup-and-silk-suit kind of way. I'm surprised I don't find her irritating and throw my drink at her. Maybe it's because I'd have to interrupt the very pleasant manicure I'm currently getting to my pitching hand.

"I've got your schedule for the day here. Would you like me to go over it with you?"

"The only schedule I ever had in my life before today was my classes at community college, and I never went to any of those even though I paid good money for them."

She don't take offense. She don't act like she even heard me. "You've got make-up and wardrobe in a half an hour, then photos with the director, Alice..."

"No photos with Alice."

"Right. Nix Alice."

I like the sound of that "nix" on Alice. She draws a line through Alice's name and goes on.

"We should really film you on the set-up here. This location is right up there with the Taj Mahal, San Simeon..."

"All ruined by tourists."

"The beauty is not the half of it Rose. I don't know what's in the water, but my hair hasn't been this silky since I was seven, and my skin positively glows. This planet is a fountain of youth."

I didn't do commercial auditions for six years without learning to pick up a cue when I hear it. "I know. But it has to be a secret. We don't want tourists to find out about this, or we'll be overrun, and then people would set up souvenir shops with bobble-head blobs and pink scarves printed with all the sights." I lean in like we're BFFs dishing a secret. "So can we keep it a secret?" I lean in closer. "Our secret."

"The only way to keep something this good a secret is to make sure only the ultra-rich have access."

"Ah, but who has the access to get the ultra-rich interested?"

Now she smiles like she just pulled a coup of a small country where she'll be the power behind the throne. She hands me her business card. "You leave that to me."

"It'll be expensive, Ellen." See, by using her first name, I'm telling her we're in business.

"It better be, Rose. More than expensive."

Ellen hurries off, her own lackeys in tow, and she's firing instructions like a sharpshooter in a pigeon coop. I'm sipping my sparkly beverage while the manicurist moves on to my left hand and I'm wondering if she does pedicures when a Blob dressed in a reptile suit interrupts my blissful bask in the sun and pulls of his mask.

"Rose, these suits are like coffins. Can't I just take it off and shape-change when nobody's looking?"

I can't believe he said that in front of one of the Hollywood humans. I turn to the manicurist. "Would you excuse us for a minute?"

She looks at me and shakes her head, mumbling something in a language I don't speak, so I guess we're safe. I glare at the offending Blob. "No."

"Why not?"

"Because I said so. You'll do as you're told."

"Why should I?"

"The fate of the planet depends on it."

"This is no fun. You promised it would be fun."

"Grow up."

"You're starting to sound like them." He walks away in a huff, and I realize a reptile huff is more funny than scary and make a note to myself to warn the director right after I take a little post-manicure siesta.

I'm about to doze off when a voice whispers in my ear, "Don't let your guard down, Madam Ambassador. The chairs here will kill you." It's Griswald, and he walks away whistling in obvious fake innocence like he didn't just say something bat-shit crazy. He's dressed in a Presidential blue suit flanked by two Secret Service Ken dolls also wearing dark glasses.

I see Ronnie wander in with her usual quivering shapeless mess, only now she's wearing a kind of lei of pretty flowers and a grass skirt. It is so wrong in so many ways that I can't help waving her over and saying so.

"I don't know how you came up with this outfit, but your shining pinkness is made so much more disgusting by your costume that it looks like matter and anti-matter is about to meet and destroy the entire space-time continuum."

"Wait till you see what I have dreamed up for the reception dinner. I'm thinking tiara and a poodle skirt."

"Maybe you could attach a page-boy hairstyle to the tiara, you know, hanging down on the sides." We both gag at the image.

"Perfect."

So we stand there contemplating ways to amuse ourselves at the expense of humanity. Griswald is prowling around the set giving sneaky jabs at the furniture and then jumping away as if it was gonna jab him back, glaring at everybody, and looking like he's contemplating some mayhem of his own.

"Say, Ronnie. What ever happened with General Griswald anyway? And why would he come back here in disguise? Does he think you don't recognize him?"

Ronnie is chuckling in little ripples that make her skirt twitch. "He came up to me the first day and introduced himself as the General's lookalike twin brother, as if we can't see his molecular structure matches down to the subatomic particles."

"So what happened the last time he was here?"

"Gaudi was worried he was taking samples. This was before the scientist types, who admitted what they were doing and so we helped them, making sure that nothing went in their test tubes that would object to being removed from the planet. But Griswald kept doing odd things, like pretending to trip and fall and then scraping up dirt under his fingernails, or coming out of the bathroom with a vial of what he claimed was his own urine so he could test his carbohydrate intake. Anyway, Gaudi went to his quarters to check it out and found he was collecting all sorts of things, from the toilet water to the stuffing of his pillows, to mouthfuls of food he obviously had chewed but not swallowed to bring them back to his room and spit into containers.

"She fiddled that stuff away and was leaving when he suddenly walked in, so she turned into a chair and figured to wait him out. Only he was suspicious of the new chair, and started muttering to himself wondering if it was a bomb, or if there were bugs in it. Then he started poking the chair with a hanger while holding a pillow in front of his chest, I guess in case it exploded. The whole think was making her laugh, and then with the poking, it also tickled, and she was moments from losing the chair shape and turning back into a Gaudi puddle, so she started to inch toward the door, figuring that to explain a walking chair was less awkward than being caught as a snoop.

"Griswald, though, went ballistic, literally. He grabbed his gun and fired six shots into the chair. Now Gaudi thought maybe he was playing, because shooting someone in your bedroom is just rude. So either way, she shot the bullets back out at him, and he keeled over bleeding. We didn't know at that time you humans couldn't just reconfigure yourselves like a normal person.

"Anyway, we patched him up like new and put him to bed in his pajamas. But when he woke up, he wouldn't calm down, figured he'd been unconscious for as long as it would have taken his body to heal on its own, and became convinced we must have done "alien experiments' on him while he slept. We rang his people to come get him. What else could we do?"

"So why is he back here?"

"Rose, do I look like I can understand the workings of a deranged mind?"

I'm looking at a pink Blob in a grass skirt, so I diplomatically avoid answering the question and bring up what to me is your salient point. "Lichtendorfman. He's got some sort of holocaust up his sleeve, and Griswald is just the fanatic to press the button. If we could just find the button."

"Quiet on the set! Places for Scene 6." The Assistant Director is a walking example of Small Man Syndrome overcompensation. He's got six walkie talkies strapped around his waist, his belt buckle belongs on a welterweight champion, his pants are too tight in the crotch, revealing that his junk is on par with the shot for Little Aldo's BB gun ammo, and he's accessorized his ensemble with a Stetson hat, lariat tie, and three-inch-heel cowboy boots. He wanders off like some town crier happily calling people to gather in the town square for a hanging.

Gaudi gives me a wave as she rolls off to find her mark, leaving me to ponder the Griswald problem all by my lonesome.

Alice is standing off by her trailer, one of four imported across the stellar void, proving Hollywood has its own magic that transforms matter, in this case money into garbage. Alice is in a slinky dress with a beauty pageant sash that says "Ambassador" and chatting with a throng of rapt Blobs while the director and camera guy play with their equipment. I do my best Griswald impression and sidle over where I won't be seen eavesdropping. I can only make out a few words, but I don't need to hear everything to fill in the blanks.

"… So I…and Rose…"

The Blobs around her all laugh, their Ken- and Barbie-ness sagging and rippling like the repulsive boils of turncoat treacle I know their souls to be. Time to lance of few of those pustules, so I grab a knife off the craft services buffet, tuck it up my sleeve, and saunter over like I haven't a clue what their saying.

"...Rose threw a fit. You know how she does. Well, I certainly wasn't going to go after the thing..."

The Blobs laugh even louder in the human way, and I notice more than a few of them don't have feet no more, but just pink puddles of goo under them. Alice, she don't show that she sees me coming, but she does that vibrator-up-the-butt wiggle that is the giveaway. She laughs a bit brighter, and her voice projects just a tiny bit more so she can make sure I'm in on the joke on me.

"I mean, imagine thinking you could flush someone down the toilet. Ha, ha."

She shakes her head with amusement so's she can "accidentally" notice me standing right there.

"Oh, Rose," she says, feigning surprise and affection in another mirror-practiced move that makes me think she and Bob are perfect for each other. "I was just telling them that funny story about the time your necklace fell into the toilet."

I turn to glare at the assembled Blobs to decide which one I should stab thirty times or so, and yes, I know it won't kill them, but it will give me a smidgen of satisfaction, which is the most I can expect when Alice is around. Only dontcha know, the Blobs raise their eyebrows and wink knowingly at me, like we are all in on a joke that Alice is not. I reel as the world spins. It's like I've been cold-cocked by my heart's desire. They are not laughing at me. They are laughing at Alice.

Alice goes on.

"You'd have thought it was priceless jewels instead of cheap plastic. Pink plastic hearts, yellow stars, blue birds, and green something."

In my state of stunned confusion, I tell her "Butterflies. They were little green butterflies," like she would care.

"Rose was so funny."

All I can picture now is not my teary pathetic self being terrorized by my big sister but the string of Alice-shaped

Blobs who went down the commode screaming. "Yeah. How dumb, even for a four-year-old. Flush. Aaaah."

More laughter. We all laugh, though Alice is not laughing at the same joke as the rest of us. The Blobs are still ugly and shapeless, Alice is still a sadist, and I'm still the last person on Earth I'd want for a self, but for the moment, it's a perfect day.

Alice notices the AD signaling her. "Oh, gotta go. Time for my scene with the President."

She waggles her fingers at the assembled blobbage, and turns to knock on the trailer door. "Bob? Honey, wake up. I've got my scene with the President coming up. You'll want to watch."

Alice prances off. The Blobs heave a collective sigh of satisfaction. "What a riot.... Rose, you were right. This is great fun.... She is everything you said. And more."

As the Blobs walk away, the trailer door opens and a sleepy Bob peers out.

"Who knocked? Rose, did you want something?" He's looking down at me with those bedroom eyes. My eyes are right at crotch level, and that knife is still in my sleeve. For a moment, I consider what could happen if the two was to "accidentally" meet. But there'd be blood, dontcha know, and not only would I faint, but I'd end up getting covered with it. I'm not against having bodily fluids all over me so long as I'm awake and willing, but unconscious it seems undignified for a waitress, let alone an ambassador. I sigh.

"It was Alice. She wants you to watch her scene."

"Her highness wants a lot of things."

I can't be hearing this right. "You mean Alice?"

"Who else acts like she's doing the world a favor just by existing?"

No one dislikes Alice. Not one human male evolved enough to work his opposable thumbs has ever found one single flaw. It's like Bob has been infected with Blob-sight. Is it in the air? The water?

Of course, again you figured it out before me. It's the water. If the Blobs can change the water to fix how people look, maybe they can change how people see. I experiment.

"Bob."

"Yeah."

"Look at me. What do you see?"

"C'mon. I see you. I mean, you lost weight, you look, you know, great now. But you're still Rose."

For magic water, it is not very effective, I'm thinking. Then Bob continues, "You know.... Fun, independent, cool, wacky, smart, spunky, sexy...you."

Okay, now, this is not natural. Six positive words about yours truly, which is six more than I got out of him in the six months we was together. I mean, Bob. Beautiful, narcissistic, and totally into... "Me?"

"Say, I'm thirsty. Come on in, if you want. I need some water."

"Here. Let me get it for you."

I'm thinking if I can not only have all the Bob physical perks but have him actually in love, or at least in like, with me, well, I could definitely return the sentiment. I'm thinking life might not be the worst idea the universe ever had. I step inside and take a gander. The set-up in here is pretty sweet. Those are satin sheets on the bed. Actually, those are my satin sheets on the bed that I had to leave behind. Figures Alice would not only steal them, but be able to sweet talk her way into being allowed to bring 'em.

There's a bunch of photos on the wall of me as Ambassador, which gives me a momentary "aw, she does care," until I see that there are mustaches and beards drawn over my face in some, and then there are collage pictures of Alice's face pasted over mine in others. The TV in the corner is showing the set where Alice is being fitted with a microphone, it looks like, but I can't tell because the sound is too low.

Meanwhile, Bob is filling a glass of water from the tap. I don't want to go head-over-heels to flat-on-my-back just yet. I need to make sure. "Don't you drink the bottled stuff?"

"They brought some from Earth, but the tap water here tastes better, if you can believe it."

He downs the whole glass. He smiles dreamily at me. Rose. I'm waiting to see what comes out of his mouth. It could all still be a misunderstanding where the joke turns out to be yours truly once again.

"Rose, believe it or not, I missed you."

Okay. That does it. His mind, what there is of it, has been taken over, and he has no choice but to like me. A nibble of conscience makes me ask, "What if I told you there was something in the water making you like me?"

Bob thinks for a minute, and then pours another glass. He looks me right in the eyes and starts to drink with that sexy smirk he used when we first met. I reach for the glass.

"Give me that. I need it more than you do."

He steps up to me, and I inhale his familiar maleness. We're going on maybe a year here with your male scent always tinged with that breath mint. I gotta tell you it's a heady aroma. Change of water has not hurt his personal cologne. He's kissing me, and I know where this is going.

"Hey. This is Alice's trailer, isn't it?"

"You feel bad? You want to go to mine?"

"Not on your life."

We fall on the satin sheets, and it's like old times. I'm even considering maneuvering into once of Landlady Moss's circus poses, but Bob is halfway to the end zone and going for the touchdown and field goal in one move, so I hop to it trying to get there with him.

I'm a little bored, though, so I grab the remote and turn up the sound on the TV so I have something to occupy my mind while my body is having its slice of Bob. Alice's voice rings through, adding some spice to the proceedings. "President Hummer. You know I'd do anything for my country, but..."

"Don't worry, Rose. Captain Roman will protect you."

"I'm a simple, city girl..." and here she stops mid-sentence. I can hear confused muttering and a loud squeaking noise that is steady and getting faster all the time. Funny, but it seems to be just a second after each one of Bob's love-moves. Someone yells "Cut," and the camera swivels. One of the trailers is doing the macarena on its foundations. Bob, meanwhile, makes with a shivering moan as he climaxes, and we both feel the earth move. At the same time, the trailer on the TV gives a giant bounce, and all the tires go flat at once with a hiss.

I have no time to wonder what was happening in that other trailer. Here in Alice's love nest, Bob is lying on the floor totally spent, us having slipped off the satin sheets at some point in the proceedings. He is looking happier than I've ever seen him, relaxed and glowing, and not at all the chiseled, indifferent hunk of manhood I find so attractive. His guard is down, and all I see is a dull and ordinary boob. Even his physique don't appeal to me after the short-order-cook style of lovemaking I musta used to like but now seems *meh*.

Oh, and now he's talking. Someone save me.

"Oh God. Oh God. Rose, Rose. Where did you learn... Oh God. I've had a lot of women, I've even had you before, but it was never so...magnificent."

"Yeah. It was okay." I'm done, so I get dressed.

"Okay? No. 'Okay' is when I balled the identical twins in free fall in the first-class-cabin bathroom of the moon shuttle. That was 'okay.' This was..."

"So-so. But I'm glad you enjoyed it. Really. I gotta go." It's odd, but a part of me can't get out of here soon enough. I was never one of those "I like to cuddle" gals, but a little happy relaxation afterward used to be part of the package. Not today.

"Rose, don't go. Please." He tries to get up, but his knees is too weak and he slides back to the floor doing a pretty good impression of a Blob. "I can't even move. Oh God."

I open the door to the trailer and step outside. The entire movie crew is staring silently at this trailer, Alice's trailer. I notice the tires are flat. Must be catching. I toss 'em a wave and tell them to carry on. I'm heading somewhere, I just don't know where. I gotta think, once the brain-numbing sex hormones wear off.

A naked Bob staggers to the door behind me as I walk away. "Rose!"

Whatever.

Chapter 14

Who's Happy Now?

I'm on my bed, but not happy. I tried napping. No sleep. I try snacking, but after one bite of more than a dozen different kinds of junk food, I toss them aside. Even a bite of Ding-Dong makes me gag, and I drop it on the bed with the rest. *Aliens* is not making me so much as smile, much less laugh. I realize I have no clue. Not that I ever had a clue, but up to this moment, I at least had a clue that I was clueless. I ain't even got that now.

Thank god Mizi shows up. It occurs to me that I have started to prefer the sight of pink blobbiness to sculpted manflesh, but I never did have no taste, so I'm not surprised. Mizi's still in her Ken-shape and is carrying a big box. I also notice that, even for a plastic doll, Mizi is looking stiff.

"Here are the dailies for you to look at." And just stands there.

"Put them in, would you? Let's see how we look."

Mizi/Ken takes out the movie and puts in the dailies. "If that's everything, I'll be going."

"Watch these with me. It should be fun."

"You're the boss."

Now the idiot sits primly on the edge of the bed and doesn't look at anything. Just sits.

"Is something wrong?"

"No, nothing. What could be wrong? Everything's going according to plan. We're screwing the humans. Or at least you are."

"Are you talking about the Bob thing?"

"I have never seen the Bob-thing."

"It's pretty remarkable by human standards, still..."

"I'm very happy for you. Now, if you will excuse me..."

A thought occurs to me that I am seeing the first break in the otherwise Blob perfection. "You're jealous."

"I'm not jealous. Blobs are never jealous."

Defensive. *Score.* I am gonna milk this until I explode with lactose-intolerant gas. "You are jealous."

"Jealousy is a human trait."

"Apparently not an exclusive one. Not only that. You are jealous of Bob. Which is doubly wonderful since it was your idea."

"If you can successfully blame me for what you did in that trailer today, I will see that you are elected queen of the Blobs."

Now I'm smiling. "The water."

Mizi/Ken looks at me like I just spoke in tongues. I don't call her on it. I just explain, like if she really didn't know what I was talking about.

"You changed the water to make everybody like me."

"Whatever gave you that idea?"

"Well, all the guys are telling me I'm a babe. *Me.* If I have an idea, everybody likes it. They treat me with respect. And people said negative things about Alice, the darling of the species. Oh, and Bob, who only notices other humans if they talk about him, Bob uttered a string of compliments that would make a narcissist blush. This cannot be done without serious mind-altering chemicals."

"Rose..."

"But I've been thinking, when people like you, you have to be, like, considerate of their feelings. I'd rather they hated me so I don't have to worry about being a jerk if I want to."

"But you are a jerk."

"Exactly. Only now I'm starting to feel guilty about it."

"Good."

"Hey! You make Bob go gaga over me, what am I supposed to do? You cannot seriously expect a girl whose degree of self-control proves the existence of Absolute Zero to resist."

"Rose, I didn't do anything to the water."

"Well, Ronnie..."

"No."

"...or Gaudi..."

"No."

"...or somebody did."

"Nobody. The water's the same as it always was."

"But ..."

I woulda at that moment had an epiphany, which some people act like is a good thing, but is more like being told you are pregnant and not only didn't you get to have sex first, but you find out God is the father, which no one in their right mind is gonna believe, and you'll be stuck raising the perfect little baby Jesus whom angels will praise and, now that I think of it, should marry Alice and both of them can go to heaven without me, but right then there's a knock at the door, and Bob pokes his head in. One epiphany avoided, praise Jesus.

"Rose." He sees Mizi/Ken sitting on my bed and stops. "Oh. Hello. Rose, can I talk to you?"

"Why? We never talked before."

"Please."

"Okay, talk."

Bob looks at Mizi/Ken impatiently and does his shrug, only it don't come out right, and I realize he ain't gonna leave but he ain't gonna talk unless we are alone. Needy men should be euthanized, not listened to. But, okay, we did have sex, however indifferent, within the last hour, so I give in.

"Mizi, I think Bob wants to bare his soul."

"Are you saying you want me to go?"

"Kind of."

"Are you sure? Very sure?"

There is some weird tone in that Ken-voice that I do not like. It is part warning, which Mizi should know by now will only make me head for disaster, not away. It is also part bossypants, which is the worst attitude a trusted friend could take with me.

"Don't take that tone with me."

I grab a half-eaten cupcake and throw it at him and follow up with a handful of chips, and then pretty much every scrap of half-eaten food and near-food on the bed. Mizi/Ken does not duck even once and is soon dripping bits from head to toe. But I don't just throw. No, I spew.

"You are not my mother. She's dead, and I haven't listened to anybody tell me what I can or cannot do since they told me I could not view the corpse and I went anyway and she was dead and her skin felt like plastic and they painted her pink and she looked like you only I wish it was you instead of her because I wouldn't want to cry for you like I wanted to cry for her but couldn't so get out of here before I forget that I am a diplomat and say something I might regret."

I'm clearly done. There's no food left on the bed. Mizi/Ken turns and goes. I find a can of Cheez Whiz under the pillow and throw it at the door as it closes. Bob, who has been watching the whole thing, turns to me.

"Wow, you do the Hollywood assistant treatment like a pro."

"Bob, what do you want?"

"I keep thinking about today."

"Today is over. It's history. Move on."

"I never felt what I felt today, and I want to give something back. I want to make you feel what I felt. If it takes my whole life, Rose, I'd like to try."

"The movie's only shooting for two months. Then you'll be gone."

"Come back to Earth with us. Marry me, Rose."

"You want to marry me? Why?"

"I want to spend my life trying to make you happy."

"Happy? Me?"

Bob walks over and kisses me like it's one of those romance movies. I cannot concentrate, the word "happy" stuck in my head like a broken record. Happy. What does it mean, happy?

Bob's asking me something. "How's this?"

"Mmm. Okay." Happy. H-a-p-p-y. Yep, I can spell it.

Bob is kissing my eyelids. Does that make me happy? How the hell do I know? Now he's fondling my left breast, too. I can feel that, why can't I feel happy?

Again he's asking something. "How's this?"

"Mmm. Not so hard."

"Softer. You got it."

If kisses on the belly moving down to between her legs could make any girl happy, that would be me. So when he asks again, "How's this?" I answer, "Good. Good, I guess."

"'Good' is better than 'okay.'" I feel his weight shift and he's on top of me now. This is what I have spent much of my life since puberty wanting. "How's it now?"

"Bigger."

"Bigger? You mean harder?" Bob does what he can, and pumps away harder.

"Sorry. I was thinking of someone else."

I'm shaking my head and realize what's wrong.. "Bob. Bob!" He stops. "This 'happy' thing, I don't think I'm cut out for it."

"Rose, please, I can do this."

"I know you can. But not with me."

"You want me to stop?"

Can I really be saying I want him to actually stop? "Yeah. Yeah, you should stop."

Bob is stunned. He withdraws cuz he ain't a bad guy, not really. Then he starts to cry. "I'm washed up."

"Bob, don't cry. Oh, Jeez. You can't go by what I think."

"You don't understand. I only got this job because of you."

"What?"

"I'd never get a starring role like this without somebody pulling the strings."

"I knew that."

"You did?"

"Come on. You AND Alice both got cast."

104

"I told the UN guy seducing you would be no problem, but he wanted me to guarantee you would come back to Earth. It was his idea I ask you to marry me."

"And you went along with it?"

"Sure. As long as I wouldn't have to actually marry you once we got back."

My genetic inclination to excuse the guys and blame the gals, remember that one, rears its head once again. I'm mad at Alice. What I can't figure is if she seduced him to help the UN make me want to take Bob back just to steal him from her, or if she seduced him to be able to always say she slept with my husband. Either way, I'm gonna kill her. I tell Bob, so somebody will know the reason.

"She doesn't know about it. She thinks she's here to put a pretty face on your image."

"You two shacking up wasn't part of the UN plan?"

"Nah, that just happened. I mean, I can't go two whole weeks without sex."

"Bob, you're a heel."

"I know. I know. You sure you don't want to finish here?" He means the sex.

"No. You go on without me."

Bob nods and does whatever needs doing while I think about this whole "happy" fiasco.

Do I even know anybody who is happy? I think about my family. Nope. Those broads wouldn't know happy if it showed up as Prince Charming down on one knee saying he didn't want no prenup. All the men I dated? Miserable, and not a thing I could do would make it better. Oh, I could make it worse, and I'm good at that, which could even be why they liked me. Having somebody to blame makes "not happy" not your fault.

Ma. Ma was happy. You could see it every time she looked at me or Alice. Happy for her was simply, "There you are. I see you. That's enough for me."

Thinking must be even harder work than I thought because I sleep like a log and wake up remembering I had good dreams. Not what they were, just that they were good. Why can't memory work that way, I ask you?

Mizi/Ken comes in when I sit up, like she was waiting outside the door listening for sounds of life.

"Good morning, Gumby. Did you bring my breakfast?"

"Where's Bob?"

"I booted him. He got so sensitive and considerate. I can't have a relationship with someone like that. I'd die of boredom."

"Rose. Last night when you threw all that food at me, I felt shock, indignation, outrage, wounded pride."

"Over a few pastries and some chips?"

"Yeah. I'm so ashamed. I've been in human form so much, I'm starting to act human."

"Well, I started acting like 'em a bit too, with everybody liking me better than Alice for once. I even told someone to 'grow up,' if you can believe it."

"You at least have an excuse. You are human, after all."

See, right here, you prob'ly think we were back on track, me and Mizi. No. I hit my head with the pillow a few times before I let myself speak.

"We're doing it again. This warm-fuzzy-touchy-feely-self-examination has got to stop. Get out of human form this instant! Take the shape of a green-eyed monster, why don't you?"

Mizi nods and changes into a vicious-looking raptor "Ah. I feel better already."

I also feel my sensitive side wither now that I am not talking to something with a human man shape. "You know, all those men I knew back on earth, I don't think I ever really noticed the person inside the body, and if I did, I wouldn't have dated any of them. I'd've picked someone more... Wow, that is a lonnng tongue."

We look at each other. Mizi/Reptile lunges for me, but I'm too quick. I'm not gonna be lizard meat any time soon, not this girl. I run, knocking over furniture and tossing anything not nailed down. Heaving stuff at a monster with intent to kill sure gets all the kinks out of your system. We go around the whole apartment twice, but when Mizi/Reptile finally catches me we are back in the bedroom and fall onto the bed.

Somewhere in the middle of the lizard love, Griswald sneaks in on us. What he sees shoulda been interesting enough for him to stop and take a lesson or two, but instead it sends him running. His loss. Because what happened next was epic. Even Hollywood woulda said so.

Chapter 15

Bounce Your Boobies

It's afternoon, and I figure it's time I make another appearance on the set. There's about an hour until the dinner break, an hour being the outer limit of what I can stand watching them work. It's not the bad dialogue or the worse acting that gives me the heebie-jeebies. I grew up on that stuff, and just like your sewer rats becoming immune to just about any disease you could inject in them, unlike your laboratory rats that just keel over from a bit of bad baloney, so a child raised on American television and movies cannot be terrorized by no amount of sex, violence, or stupidity on the screen. No, what wears me out is how serious everybody takes their job and themselves.

I'd understand if it was just the half-pint Assistant Director in the ten-gallon hat. But it's all of them. The camera crew creaming over a light reflected on a hairpin like they could actually see angels dancing on it. Or the actors wandering all over going "oo-ah-oo-ee" and "red-leather-yellow-leather" like they was crazies on the ward. Or the lighting and props guys looking down the nose at everybody else cuz they can lift a few sandbags or stick a plug in an extension cord, and god forbid an ordinary person tried to turn on a light or move a candlestick so she could put her plate of nachos down someplace comfortable and nice, like the interstellar lounge bar set. Jeez.

But they are all amateurs at being "too important to shit" when it comes to the director, who I'm sure they only picked cuz he's built like a blob, being almost too wide to stand without a crane to lift him up and as soft and flabby as Gaudi herself, which shoulda made him comfortable being in a place where he kind of fit, even if he is the wrong color. But no. He hides out in his trailer and only comes out to whisper to the camera guy, or mumble to the actors, all the while looking at everyone else like they was lizard droppings.

Everybody is practicing the art of contempt, like anybody on this world cares what they think. I don't know. I guess on Earth, maybe it's different. But here, the cliquey thing just means they leave us to ourselves when there's no movie stuff going on, and so we only get bored by them in small doses instead of suicidally depressed by the bleakness of their company. And when I talk suicide, I mean in a mass-grave sort of way, cuz anybody or group of bodies who drive me to it are going with me to have a few words with the man upstairs. And yes, I do think it's a man. Would a woman create a world this pointless and broken? Not a chance.

I show up on set, and one of the peons runs and grabs my chair from over by the wall and brings it to me like she's trying to beat the Guinness Book on chair-toadying. I mean, would it be so bad if I sat in a different chair, one that had somebody else's name on it?

"Can I get you anything else, Madam Ambassador?"

"Can you get me a picture of my fourth grade teacher in front of a firing squad being riddled with bullets? No? Then forget it."

My fourth grade teacher was a nasty, miserable woman, even compared to the other elementary school teachers in my school. It made me wish for the nuns who my neighbor Maggie O'Brien used to tell me about, how they would whack the kindergarteners with a ruler for fidgeting and lecture about the horrors of hell, but hadn't made you stand up in front of class and confess to things you didn't actually do. Mrs. Grouper did that. She picked one or two "golden" kids in every class who she decided were perfect, and when they figured out they could do anything and just blame a classmate with impunity, the power would go to their heads and they became sociopaths for a year. They could accuse other students of any crime, even anatomically impossible transgressions, and she would punish the "offender" in front of the rest of the class. She never told us who her special "angel" students were to keep them "safe," but by the end of the year, kids always figured it out by process of elimination. From that year forward, they would be outcasts and scapegoats. I was not her golden child, but I did make friends with a few after they was ruined and miserable. Someday I'm sure one of them will snap, and I'll be able to say I went to school with a mass murderer.

I turn my attention back to the business of busy-ness and realize something is off. The entire cast and crew is mostly standing around waiting. Someone even yawns, and nobody fires him on the spot. The Assistant Director stalks off and knocks insistently on Alice's door.

"Miss Delancy, your needed on the set."

No answer. I coulda told him you don't get Alice to do anything without a pretty-please-with-a-cherry. The AD shrugs and goes over to confer with the director and producer. I catch Ellen Wishford's perfectly mascaraed eye and wave her over.

"What's up? Why isn't anything happening?"

"Oh, Rose. Your sister has a scene to shoot and won't come out of her trailer."

Dick Glick notices us gabbing and makes a beeline with "serious" written all over his face. I don't do serious. I don't answer to serious. And I refuse to take serious seriously.

"Rose, she's your sister. Get her out here. Right. Now."

"Dick, don't be a dick. I don't take orders from dick."

"Rose, if you don't get her over here, I'm putting that..." He points to Mizi/Reptile. "...in a gown and having it play you."

He think it's a threat. But it is the first even mildly interesting idea I've heard the guy come up with. I like to encourage the aggressive, the rash, and the ridiculous whenever I come across it, so even though I'm pissed at him for trying to order me around, I say, "Good idea."

He snorts. Not a good look on him. "You want the world to think you're a hideous reptile?"

I lean forward in my chair and jab my finger into his diamond-crusted gold peace symbol bling necklace. "Hideous reptile is better than girlie-golly!-gullible imbecile. In fact, it's the first original idea you've had on this whole stupid project." I sit back with a *hmph* as in "so there."

"I don't think..."

At this moment, I do not care if the movie works back on Earth. The bone-wearying predictability of everything that has happened on the set and around these people is not worth putting up with to save the planet. And maybe we don't even need the movie at all, now that Ellen is on board. So let him take his toys and his collection of contempt-bots, and go home. I am not holding my tongue any more. I cut him off.

"More wisdom. Dick, you're on a new planet. Make a new movie. The square-jawed captain is a boob. The President is venal and depraved. The cute girl is evil down to her twisted DNA. The aliens are good and pure until the humans come, then they start becoming reflections of the humans: evil, boob-ish and depraved all at once. Food and sex orgies..."

"Sex orgies? I'm listening." You gotta hand it to the guy. He don't take nothing personal if he sees dollar signs in it.

Ellen, though, she is concerned about her own dollar signs. "But what about the spa? I thought this movie was to advertise the spa."

"Advertising is the cocaine of the mass media. Do we want the masses here?

"Heavens no! But still..."

I hold up my hand and turn to Glick. "Dick, tell me. If we made this planet a spa you could visit, would people with money pay to come or not?

"A spa? I could stay after the movie shoots?"

"You'd have to pay."

"I'm losing weight without dieting. The bags under my eyes are gone. And my hair is growing back in. I'll pay whatever you're asking."

I look over at Ellen who is nodding and smiling. "Case closed." This time I lean sideways toward Dick so it feels more chummy. "Now let's call a break. You go write a script that is everything you cannot do in a space movie."

"Okay, sure. It might even be fun for once. Everything but comedy. You can't make a sci-fi comedy."

A comedy sounds about right to me, but before I can argue, Griswald charges onto the set in wielding an axe. He heads straight for Mizi in her Reptile suit, axe held high. I smile and holler, "Bounce!"

Mizi gets the message. Everyone gasps as Griswald swings the axe down onto its head with all he's got. "Rape our women, you fiend! I'll kill you!"

The axe hits square on the noggin, smooshes in, and bounces back so fast that Griswald ends up on his behind. Everyone laughs.

Griswald, the sap, keeps getting back on his feet, swinging harder each time. And every time, the axe bounces, taking him with it. The laughter finally gets through to Griswald. He looks around him. "You can take over everyone else's mind, but I will die a free man."

With a desperate gleam in his eye, he turns the axe around and makes to use it on himself. Again I holler, "The axe!" The humans think I'm calling to have someone take it away from Griswald, but the Blobs know exactly what I mean. The axe hits his head and it bends like a rubber bat, then bounces back, flying out of his hands and lands at Mizi's feet. Ever helpful, Reptile Mizi picks it up and hands it back to Griswald. Griswald takes it, sighs, and wanders off. Everyone on the set applauds.

Dick is watching them laugh. I give him a nudge. "A sci-fi comedy. Go write it. The Blobs will fix the scenery. After lunch we reconvene."

"What about Alice?"

"I'll handle Alice. Go."

They hurry off. Mizi sidles over. "Did I hear you say you'd handle Alice?"

I don't know what came over me, but I figure, what can it hurt to try? I go over to Alice's trailer, sit on the steps and call out loud enough to be heard inside. "Alice. So you're giving up, admitting I won? Say it. I want you to say it: 'You win.' How many times have you made me say it. Well, now it's my turn, and if you have an ounce of pride, you'll say it to my face."

No answer. That's okay. I'm just warming up here.

"Well, I always suspected you would turn out to be a coward if the tables ever turned. I guess I was right."

The door opens behind me and there's Alice standing in the semi-dark, no make-up, ratty hair, and with eyes puffy like she's been crying. I say nothing, just raise my eyebrow as in, "Well? I'm waiting." And dontcha know, she caves.

"You win."

I take a deep breath of satisfaction, ready for the sweet taste of victory, but all I get is a feeling like halitosis of the heart. I musta mis-heard, or misunderstood. "Alice, say it again."

"You win. You win, you win, you win, you win. Are you satisfied?" She even stomps her foot, and it's not a calculated stomp, it's a six-year-old don't-want-to-stand-in-the-corner stomp. I do not want to win over a six-year-old. I am not satisfied, not in the littlest bit.

While I ponder the difference between hope and reality, Alice has noticed that everyone is gone from the set.

"Where is everybody?"

"They broke early. We're changing the script, rewriting the whole story."

"And writing me out, I bet. Out of everything. Fine. I won't stay where I'm not wanted." Alice jumps past me and starts walking away.

"Actually not... Hey, Alice! Where are you going? There's nothing out there."

Alice does not answer. She's got her head high, and she's walking without a clue where she's going or what will happen when she gets there. She reminds me of me.

"Alice! Don't be a dope!"

I haul myself up and start after her. So she starts to run. Oh goody. I gotta run if I want to keep her in sight. She takes the path to the [*spitting-choking-word*] baths. I do not want her to fall in, have all her skin stripped off, and have everybody blame me for it. Not that I care what everybody else thinks, but I'd maybe agree with them on this one, and if I agreed with the world on one thing, I might lose the ability to ignore them on everything else. I pour on the speed as she makes the turn to go up instead of down, which is one catastrophe averted. We reach the top almost at the same time, and Alice runs right up to the edge before turning.

"Stay back! Stay back, or I'll jump."

It's a long way down, too long. I myself never lived in an apartment above the fifth floor, in case I ever got too depressed with the thought of how life just goes on and on all by itself. Any higher, and your chances of dying after a jump are pretty good, in which case your troubles would be over. Lower, though, and jumping might only crush your spine and there you'd be, still alive but now crippled or deformed, which is something I would not risk no matter how depressed a girl I was. Here, it's way more than five stories up, so I do not want to do or say anything to push her. Which is a surprise for me. I consider the reverse psychology approach, you know, telling her to go ahead and jump so's she won't. Only the tiny chance that she actually might on my say-so stops me. The problem is, if I'm not being my natural rude self, I got nothing but clichés.

"Alice, come away from there. Come on. Give me your hand…"

"I'm not giving you anything. I've been trying my whole life to get back everything you stole from me."

"What did I ever steal from you? As far back as I can remember, Alice, it was you taking from me."

"Just because you don't remember, doesn't mean it didn't happen."

"What did I do?"

"You were born."

"Hello, not much I could do about that."

"I wanted a sister or brother. I was looking forward to it. But from the day you arrived, I was suddenly not good enough."

"Are you crazy? Everybody adored you. They treated you like a princess and me like the frog."

"Oh, yeah, everybody who didn't matter, patting me on the head, dressing me up, suffocating me till I wanted to scream. I hated them, but they were all I had."

"What are you talking about?"

"Ma. Ma changed. I was pretty, and cute, and perfect, and she loved you so much more than she loved me, I wanted to die. Instead she died, and there I was, supposed to be the big sister and take care of you when all I wanted to do was drown you in the bathtub and say a burglar came in and I hid and you screamed and to keep you quiet he pushed you under the water. I even took Aunt Mizi's gold watch and opal earrings once and hid them so the story would be more believable."

"You really thought it out, didn't you?"

"But I couldn't, so I killed your fish instead."

"You killed Goldie! I thought I killed Goldie."

"I dumped out the fish food and put sawdust in the box.

"You bitch. I loved that fish!"

Suddenly, all the years of torture come back to me and float like the vision of Goldie dead jumbled with waxy skin in a funeral home and pink hearts in the toilet. I leap and grab her hair and, honest to god, for a minute I feel the strength to tear it all out at the roots. But Alice, she digs her fingernails into my cheeks and I'm slapping her hands away. Then she's slapping mine and we're like playing cards in the wheels of a bicycle.

"Fish murderer!"

"Boyfriend stealer!"

"He was my boyfriend first!"

"She was my mother first!"

We fall to the floor and now we're both trying to get on top and strangle the other. First my head, then her head hangs over the edge. Suddenly I have a thought.

"Wait. Wait. What about Pop?"

Alice stops digging her thumbs into my throat. "What about him?"

"Who did he love most? You or me?"

"Pop? He didn't love either one of us. He loved Pop."

There we are, maybe ten stories up on the edge of a tower on a planet light years from New Jersey, an entirely new place, but we might as well be in the basement of our duplex in Nutley right now. And like back then when we used to fight, it turns and we start to laugh. I forgot that part until just now, but when we was kids we'd fight and five minutes later, we'd laugh. Somewhere along the way we got too serious, and the fighting was all there was.

Alice rolls off me, and we both sit with our legs dangling over the edge laughing. "Mom had terrible taste in men."

"So do I."

"Me too."

"Clearly, since we both picked the same one."

"You can have him back if you want. He makes smooching noises when he kisses. I can't stand that."

"I don't want him. He's a weasel. He's working for the UN trying to trick me into going back to Earth."

"You don't want to go home?"

"Home? I know it sounds crazy, but I am home."

And it's true. I like it here. I'm almost afraid to say it, afraid that saying it will jinx it or attract the attention of the hope-stealers and dream-breakers all climbing their way to a fantasy world of success and power. This place, though, it's real, and I decide right there to have a little faith in it, in the Blobs. In me.

Oh heck. And Alice.

I'm shaking my head at myself for my ridiculous confidence that it's all going to be alright. The landscape stretches out before us in a spectacular display of gentle and graceful beauty.

"It's a great place."

"And I plan to keep it that way."

"Then why the movie?"

"I thought if we became a spa for the rich and famous, the UN couldn't launch a takeover or strip-mining operation, or reservation for the Blobs to live while builders put in planned vacation communities and malls. The movie was just to get to the right kind of people who could tell the rest of the world to keep their paws off it."

"A spa world. Great idea."

"Yeah, but I do not have the temperament to host the thing. I'm too cranky."

"Rose, is the landscape trying to say something?"

"I don't know. It does that sometimes."

We both shut it for a while, and sure enough, on Bliss, when you look at the world with your heart open, the whole world speaks to you in a language you can understand. Both me and Alice, we crack a smile at the same time.

"What a great idea."

We're standing up, and Alice's foot slips. I grab her, but we're off balance and we pitch over the edge. Simultaneously, we both scream, "Nooooooo!" It's far enough I have time to realize that if we're both gonna die, I can at least have the last word, so I call out to her "You owe me a Coke!" but dontcha know, she says the exact same thing to me at the same time. I guess there's no winning with Alice, but winning's overrated. I reach out for her hand, and she takes mine.

It is a long fall, but at the bottom we don't exactly hit and go splat, cuz the ground smooshes like a trampoline. We slow down and then stop for a second, and then we're heading back up faster and faster until the rebound throws us back into the air. We're screaming again, but this time like we was at Coney Island on the best ride ever. Somersaults and belly flops, landing on our feet or landing on our heads, we hold hands and realize nothing can hurt us but each other, and that ain't happening again, not in this lifetime.

Chapter 16
The Plot Thins

It's a new day on Bliss, and a new movie is in the works. The scenery is now wildly alien in a Buck-Rogers-on-LSD kind of way. Alice in a virginal white dress is standing over the tied-up Bob in a space captain suit. She is holding a knife. Bob as the Captain struggles against the ropes.

"Quick, Rose. Take the knife and cut me loose before the aliens come and eat my penis."

"Gee, captain. I'm not sure I know how to use a knife. I'm just a girl. Knives, space ships, guns, trains, those are boy things."

Griswald, as the UN Secretary General, comes in, followed by several Blobs in their normal pink shapelessness, though Mizi is sporting a handlebar mustache. Alice hides the knife behind her back and stands with her head down in a demure, submissive pose.

Griswald/Secretary General signals to the Blobs. "There he is. Take him away."

Bob/Captain cries out, "No. No. Leave me my manhood."

Mizi turns to Griswald. "Mr. Secretary, we're tired of killing and eating people. Can't we go shopping or something?"

"He's the last one. Then you can rest."

"What about the girl?"

"Leave her to me."

With a theatrical sigh of resignation, the Blobs drag away a weeping and pleading Bob/Captain.

Griswald walks over to Alice and tips her chin up to look him in the eye. "Well, Rose. What will it be? Truth and justice, or the American way?"

"Oh, the American way, always. Now that the Captain is out of the way, I was wondering if you would maybe let me have his ship. As a present for helping you."

"No, no Rose. My plan is to fly the ship back to Earth single-handed and describe how the horrible violent aliens killed all the valiant noble Earth men and raped the beautiful ambassador and then we'll lead an armada to destroy their filthy race to the last pink marshmallow and set up some factories that don't need to worry about pollution or toxic waste..."

"But... Nobody's raped me, sir."

"Not yet."

Griswald reaches to rip off her bodice, pulls her into his arms, and kisses her violently. She throws her arms around him and, with the knife still in her hand, stabs him in the back.

"Aaggh. Who would have thought a sweet little girl like you..."

He staggers and falls to his knees, the knife still imbedded. Mizi returns as Griswald reaches into his pocket and pulls out a remote. "I may be done for, but I'm taking the lot of you with me. This will detonate all the arms depots all over the planet, cracking this world like an egg. See who has the last laugh."

He proceeds to laugh maniacally as he presses the button, but his laughter dies away when nothing happens. After a moment, Mizi belches. Griswald hits the button again, and again a large belch from Mizi is all that happens.

Mizi looks down at Griswald, "About those arms depots. They were a bit spicy, but otherwise quite tasty."

Alice/Rose peels the fake mustache off Mizi and takes a paw. "You ate the bombs?"

Mizi nods. "It seemed like a good idea at the time."

Griswald jams the button a few more times, but all he gets is a long series of belches out of Mizi. Griswald dies with a wail of despair. Mizi pats his tummy as Alice sighs contentedly. "There's no place like home."

Mizi puts an appendage arm around her shoulder and they walk off into the sunset.

The director cries, "Cut. That's a wrap!"

The director is a good 50 pounds lighter, and the loss of weight has likewise lightened his mood. Or maybe it's the water. Whatever, the whole lot of us, cast, crew, Blobs, and yours truly, bust into applause. Alice, she curtsies and gestures to me to take a bow myself, to another round of cheers. I confess I am still a little confused every time she is nice to me, but I will just have to get used to it since the planet thinks she should stay.

So life on the Unpronounceable Spa of Bliss, or the Bliss Spa of Unpronounceable, or as I call it, home, settles into a regular pattern. Alice, like the landscape suggested, runs the spa. Very rich people who are puffy, balding, and wrinkled arrive and are met by Ken and Barbie Blobs. Meanwhile, equally rich people who are sleek, elegantly coiffed with glowing skin transfer funds to Ronnie's account in Switzerland before they depart for the space ship.

Lichtendorfman doesn't work at the UN no more. Blob Alice took his job. Now she's doing all kinds of nefarious deals on Earth, and so long as she don't meddle with life here, she don't get called back by the "government" on Bliss. Which is fine by her, cuz the less she thinks about this place, the better.

I hope she's as happy there as I am here. Yes happy. Not the kind of happy that Bob was talking about. Not even the kind of happy I thought happy was for most of my life. Happy is just not afraid to care and being yourself no matter what.

I kinda put Blob Alice in touch with the real Aunt Mizi, who took one look at her pink fakeness and recognized a kindred spirit. At least she stopped pestering me and Alice to let her come live with us here. Maybe she's even happy now. I think old Mizi hated being nobody and likes being a rich some-body, thanks to us sending her part of the money we make here. I mean, money's no use to us, but if we don't charge extortionist rates to come to Bliss, then we'd be overrun, and overrun is not how we like things. We like it with Earth and humans over there, and the Blobs plus a select few over here.

Now the only problem, still in the distant future, is a matter of biology that I blame entirely on Mizi. Somehow, yours truly has gotten in the family way. At first I wondered if it coulda been Bob, but no man has sperm that last two months before surprising that one lucky egg. No, it was Mizi and that "replicating human form down to the molecular level" that did it, which means only pink Blob form or green-eyed monsters having sex with Rose henceforward. Nothing close enough to human to fertilize an egg, which is fine by me anyway, me and Mizi having made our way through the entire roster of cultural icons and idols leaving me kind of done with manly-for-manly-sake. Friendly alien sex is good enough for this girl from Jersey.

At the moment, Mizi is reading another child-rearing book à la Dr. Spock. "You humans do this to your children? No wonder they grow up insane."

"Everything in that book was done to me, and I turned out alright."

"Correct me if I'm wrong, but you turned into a social misfit who got herself pregnant by an alien life form…"

"Hey! You should've explained that the inner biology adjustment you was making included sperm."

"…who lives only for pleasure and expresses love by throwing things at the object of her adoration."

I grab one of the books off the pile and chuck it at him. I'm calling Mizi "him" for now because getting a girl pregnant qualifies, I figure. He ducks.

"Case in point."

"So what are you saying?"

"I'm saying we do everything exactly as the book says."

See, this is why I'm still here. I'm me and that's okay with both of us. I can forgive errors on the molecular level, since who understands space-time anyway. Side note, Einstein was one of the more fun icons to have sex with, having wild hair that on Unpronounceable has a mind of its own.

Lost in my Einstein mental time warp, it takes me a minute to notice that Mizi has stopped reading. I look up, and he explains. "This book says to keep the pregnant mother happy, to give her gifts and compliments and massages and such so the chemicals in her blood are optimal for the growing fetus."

"So am I getting a gift, a massage, a compliment, or a such?"

"Which one do you want right now?"

Now you know how much I've changed, because I say the thing I want. Trust, it changes your life. I'm a gal who has everything she ever needed or wanted, but I don't let that stop me. "Gift."

Mizi opens his hand, okay, pink paw, and in it is a necklace. It's a necklace made of colored plastic: pink hearts, yellow stars, blue birds, and green butterflies. It's the most beautiful thing I ever saw.

"Alice helped me get the shapes and colors right."

"You give a grown woman pregnant with your child a cheap plastic necklace?" Those are not tears in my eyes. The plastic reflects the sun too bright, dontcha know. "You are insane."

Mizi puts it on me. "Of course. Who else would put up with you?"

"Okay, just for that crack, I am never having sex with you again."

"Oh no? How about a dance?"

Mizi suddenly turns into a young Jimmy Stewart in black-and-white doing a Charleston knee-wobble move. He grabs my hand, and we're hopping forward and backward on the wood floor of a big old high-school gym as the music blares. Yes, *It's a Wonderful Life*. Who doesn't know what comes next? I smile.

"I hate you."

"I know."

The floor opens up, and we fall into the swimming pool underneath, but he never stops dancing. Neither do I.

Author Biography

Susan diRende ran away from college and joined the circus at 20 where she learned how to step outside the boundaries just far enough to get a laugh. Ever since then, she has been writing, painting, performing, and directing with the goal of bringing about illumination and transformation through laughter. In 2005, she founded the Broad Humor Film Festival to support women's comedic vision on film and ran it for the first 9 years, when it was named one of the 5 top film festivals for women in the world. In 2015, she sold most of her belongings, packed up the rest, and hit the road for a vagabond lifestyle.

sudirende.tumblr.com